Dreamweavers Awakening

Stanley L. Garland Jr.

Contents

Chapter 1

Where am I? What is this bright light? He was surrounded in darkness, distant thoughts he knew were important flickered at the edge of his mind. *What are they? So far away...* A hazy white started to come to him.

"Oh, you're awake. If I waited any longer, excessive measures were an alternative," a female voice spoke.

Blinking, he tried to bring the world around him into focus. "Who?" He winced, still blinking, lifting an arm up to block some of the light unsuccessfully. "What are you?" the male voice asked.

"Oh, Sean, I'm your Guardian Angel. Welcome to the afterlife." The voice warmed as it spoke.

"The afterlife? Where is Tabatha?" *I can't even remember.* He rubbed his eyes, still attempting to get them to work.

"Tabatha? That is your past, and we need to concentrate on the present," Sean finally got his eyes to focus enough to catch the Angel's gentle smile.

Sean sat up in the bed, letting the cover slide down his chest and pool by his left arm. He looked around the tiny white room. Lifting his gaze past the pristine white walls, there was a midsized rectangular window that stood vertically, giving him a small peek into the world beyond the room. Outside the window was a crystal, near emerald-blue ocean that had waves cresting and shimmering

1

beyond his reach. The smell of the salty water was refreshing in the sterile environment. Though if he were to be stuck in this place with only the view and the scent, in time, it could drive a man nuts... *Didn't she say something about after life?* Did he go to a place of torment? No, no, he must be in a hospital room... without equipment... He turned his attention to the woman standing at his bedside. She appeared to be seven feet tall, and her wings were tucked behind her gray business suit. *Aww, a lawyer... there must have been an accident...*

"Nice wings." The compliment escaped his mouth without thinking. Turning his head to look himself over, seeing if he could find the reason he was here. "So, what happened? Are you here to help me with a case so I could get some cash..." He trailed off, frozen for a couple of beats as his mind started to try and reason through what he knew and had seen. *Wings, afterlife, didn't she say something about being an angel?* Lifting his head to eye her, he swallowed. "So..." He licked his lips sucking them gently. "You're my Guardian Angel?" He waited a beat to see if she would react like any sane person on Earth would, but she just stood there calmly and composed. "But You, you—look like a 1980s businesswoman!" He gestured widely at her clothing. "Why are you wearing a power suit?" Sean's eyes furrowed as he waited for her answer. *Maybe this is a wild dream... yeah, a dream.. what did I have for dinner last night? Steak, wine, mashed potatoes... maybe a wild dream... Wake up, wake up, wake up!*

"What's with the snarky look? The Goddess Anastasia told me I could pick any outfit I want." The angel crossed her arms, and if Sean didn't know any better, he would say that she was almost pouting. "This one spoke to me…" She whipped her head around to look at him, sending her cotton candy traces fluttering. "Don't make fun of it." Sighing and letting the tension drop out of her shoulders, she then winked at Sean and smiled before twirling slowly.

Sean shook his head for a moment, his thoughts racing. He was still here… not a dream then. So he didn't want to start negative… "I'm in the afterlife?" He gripped the blanket to give him some sense of security. "Am I in heaven, paradise…" His grip tightened. "Or somewhere else?" It was taking everything he had to remain calm.

"You're in none of the above." Her voice was smooth and clear, a tone that suggested she was not playing a joke on him… she seemed serious. "You are in a spiritual battleground." The angel stood upright, towering over him, and locked her caramel orbs onto his hazel ones.

"A spiritual battleground," Sean parroted softly.

"Yes." Samantha nodded. Her right hand reached over toward her left as she fidgeted with the purple metal charms that rested there. "Right now, we're in between the realm of Heaven and Earth. Anastasia created a checkpoint here for us to fight the demons." Her delicate fingers traced one of the star-shaped charms, the light catching it and reflecting from the gem therein… it was dazzling. "For you to make it to the afterlife, you have a choice to make."

"A choice?" Sean stared, mouth hanging open. There was no choice; he had to go back! "I was about to propose to my girlfriend.

The stage was set." He lifted a hand to his head and rubbed his temples, hiding his eyes, and he tried to calm himself... "What happened? I need to know," Sean persisted.

"In time you will understand." She dropped her right hand back by her side before gesturing upward. "Do you want to go to Pardise?" Moving her hand out to the side she asked, "Do you want a second chance?" The angel looked sternly at Sean.

Sean shifted as he rose up more in the bed. It caused the white blanket to slide more to the left, revealing his black and red plaid jammie pants that did not in any way match his blue dolphin shirt. Sean paused in his movement, realizing he couldn't just go.... Another realization popped into his head; he didn't even know what to call her... "First of all, what's your name? You look like you can handle yourself." His eyes traced the sword on her hip, which mirrored the length of his body. "You could impale me before I even move."

"As your Guardian Angel, I am given certain powers by Anastasia to kill demons, but yes, if it means keeping you in this room, I could kill you ten times over and send your soul away." The angel put her hand on the hilt of her sword tilting it. "Like I said, this is a new spiritual testing ground. We are trying to see if humans can be redeemed a different way."

"When you say redeemed, you mean a different way other than Anastasia?" Sean looked at the angel cautious, trying to decide whether he could make a break for the door.

"No." She shook her head. "Anastasia is still the one and true way to redemption. Humans reject her. This experiment, or shall I say the new mission is to give humans a different chance at improvement." Turning her head away slightly, she looked at Sean out of the corner of her eyes. "I will say no more." The angel put her left arm out the purple and gem stone covered star charm bracelet swayed with movement as she used her right hand to brush off an imaginary critter or dust from her clothing. "What is your choice?"

Sean frowned, his eyes sliding to the door and back to her. "First your name, then choice." Sean crossed his arms, appearing unfazed by her persistence.

The angel frowned a bit. "My name is irrelevant, your choice?"

Sean shook his head. "I need your name before I can answer." He wasn't about to budge on this.

"Human!" She drove her right leg into the ground shaking the room violently. "My patience grows thin. My name cannot be pronounced by your tongue. You can call me Samantha."

Smirking, Sean rose up and took her left hand in his bringing it up to his lips, "What a pretty name," Sean said.

Samantha pulled her hand back as if she had been burned. "That charm of yours is ever-growing. People were enamored by you." She looked at him and his mix-matched clothing. "You could have done great things on Earth. The party lifestyle you adopted ruined you. All of those low-income jobs. Your parents paid for your

Roth IRA. They also made sure you had a place to stay. Your mom worried all the time." She eyed him sharply. "Shall I go on?"

Sean shrugged his shoulders rolling them forward. "Brilliance takes time to produce. Don't people party in hell?" Sean looked at the angel with a mischievous grin.

Samantha snapped her fingers as screams filled the room.

The young man put his fingers cupping his ears. "Make it stop!" Sean bellowed.

Samantha snapped her fingers as the screams dissipated from the room. "Hell is not an endless party. You cannot have sex when you want. You are tortured from now to the end of time. Most humans would have decided by now. You have ten seconds, or you will be cast into The Void."

"Okay, okay, whatever you want me to do, I agree to it," Sean said. "Don't let me hear those screams ever again. I heard a person say they were pulling out their fingernails. One woman had her eyes gouged out. She was naked and being raped by some sort of demon." Sean laid face down on the bed, his head buried into the sheet. "It sounded awful. Please have mercy. I will do whatever it takes."

"That is a good choice." Samantha clapped her hands twice, turning around. "Anastasia does have mercy on humans. There are occasions where we must scare you into the right decision. I'm sorry I had to show you the other side. Your free will is also your greatest fall. What are you waiting for?"

Sean lifted his head. Putting his legs over the side of the bed, he cautiously stood up. His body felt lighter than usual. It was a weird sensation. If he could describe it, it would be like being on the moon but with weights on his arms and legs. He jumped for a moment and felt like he jumped twice high as he could on Earth. It wasn't quite what people described the afterlife to be. He was scared, but he knew The Void was not a place he wanted to go.

Samantha walked forward, her wings tucked behind her back, opening the door before her. "Sean, welcome to the Dreamweaver's Society."

Sean stepped through the door. His eyes surveyed books on shelves high as the eye could see. He saw people of all sizes and angels that looked like humans with supernatural abilities. They were floating flawlessly, pulling books out and putting them back on the shelves at an alarming rate.

"Humans are dying at a rapid rate, and we don't have enough time to process them all. Why can't we get some help here?" An older angel with a double chin floated above them grabbing a book quickly scrolling through its contents.

Samantha walked by, looking at the angel who shouted. "You know most of the warrior angels are fighting advance level demons. We don't have angels to put toward this project."

The older angel glided toward Samantha. He had a dwarf like appearance with a long beard. "You speak the truth, but it's hard to keep up with how fast they are coming in. We can't catch them all and some of them are going straight to The Void without a chance." He put his wrinkled finger up pointing it at Sean. "Like that one. I saw your conversation through the observation mirror. He almost didn't make it."

Sean looked up and at the pint-size creature. "You're one to talk; you barely come to my waist." He put his hand on his hips, bending over his eyes glaring down at the angel.

Samantha put her hands up, slapping them tougher as if brushing off dust from a good cleaning. "Ignore him. He's confused. I am taking him to the briefing room so he can understand what all of this is about."

"Hope so. Alexis can put him into shape. I hate being here, and she dragged us with her." The grumpy angel twitched his neck to Sean. "I miss the cooks in paradise. These chefs here are good but I consider them rejects."

"They're not that bad," she stated, turning away from him smiling. Samantha waved her right hand, continuing down the long path.

Sean put his hands in his pockets and gave the angel a head nod. He followed Samantha out of the extensive library area. So, this area is where people are processed. "Those doors connect to the world or our subconscious?"

"At the moment, it is beyond your comprehension," Samantha said. "Alexis, who's in charge of the program, will enlighten you. There is no turning back. This is your path to redemption, and don't blow it." Samantha opened the door, and they walked out into a giant mall of sorts.

There were shops and stores with people running to and fro.

"This looks like where I'm from. What is this?" Sean looked bewildered as they walked, noticing escalators and stairs and people flying. If there are people with magical abilities on display, why do they take contraptions like elevators or stairs for a situation instead of flying?

"Guardian Angels want to feel close to you. We want to know what it is to live in your shoes. We were created by Anastasia, so our existence is different. We have lots of power. But you were made in the image of Anastasia, which was different from how we were made. So for us to best relate to you, we dress like you and created a home similar to yours."

Sean nodded closely, following Samantha. He saw what appeared to be clothing stores, entertainment facilities. There was also music playing. It sounded like rock music with harps and violins. It was a unique sound that he'd never heard before. "From what I gather, this looks like a hangout spot for humans. You said welcome to the Dreamweaver Society. What is a Dreamweaver? Are all of these people Dreamweavers?"

"You do catch on," Samantha said, looking back at the tiny human behind her with a smile. "You were always intuitive when I watched you as a young child. Why didnt you become an engineer?"

"The old man pushed a lot on me. He wanted me to be good at everything. I got tired of it. I still do have a knack for that skillset." Sean looked at the ground, thinking about his father, who died before he could see him reach his full potential.

"I'm not going to show you all of our society, but the door we're about to go through leads out to the extraordinary chambers to where Alexis resides. You will do well to mind your manners. She holds the key to your salvation and your success here."

Sean nodded, taking a big gulp as two large golden doors open to a brilliant staircase with large pillars on each side. He could barely comprehend what was before him. The physics of the earth played no part in the supernatural area. When the doors closed behind him, it looked like he was walking in the clouds, the stairs were translucent, and he stepped up beside his Guardian Angel.

"Continue onward," a loud voice said.

"She sounds scary," Sean whispered, looking over at his Guardian Angel.

"She's only scary if you get on her bad side. She is a loving angel, but she has a limit. Thankfully I'm one of her favorites, so everything should be well."

Sean nodded as he continued to walk up the stairs. He came to the top; it appeared to be large golden drapes and velvet chairs everywhere. They were three maids cleaning up the room, and a desk with an oversized chair turned toward the bookshelf behind where the influential voice echoed.

"You must be the new recruit," the voice said. "So, you say you want to earn your salvation back. You didn't seem so sure when you talked to Samantha."

"Alexis." Sean let out a small squeak as he faced the woman in front of him. "I was nervous and scared. I still am. I have no idea what's happening to me; I know I feel safe, and I followed Samantha here to you. My eyes cannot comprehend what I see. If you could please give me guidance and wisdom, I would greatly appreciate it."

"So, you do have potential." Alexis swung around to reveal her small stature. She appeared to be three feet tall, and beside her, a staff golden in color with the initials A on it.

Sean tried to keep in his laughter, his cheeks flared red. He turned around. "Though I need to keep my composure, I don't want to be sent to hell for laughing at the leader of this domain. I could be dreaming in hell if I'm not careful."

"Are you done? I could send you to The Void for that. I know my small stature elicits a certain reaction from your kind, but I am a high-ranking angel, and with a snap of the finger, you could be turned into dust. So do not mock me again."

Sean, looking over at Samantha, wanting comfort.

Samantha stared forward, her blue eyes looking at the bookshelf behind Sean, paying no mind to Sean's antics. "Alexis, Sean would like the ability to become a Dreamweaver?"

"If I may ask, what does a Dreamweaver do?"

Alexis sat back in her chair, looking at the man before her. "Dreamweaver's here in our society are those individuals with special privileges to enter the dreams of humans on Earth. You would be, as you would say it in your language, a ghost. People with high spiritual nature may be able to see you. But you go out at night on missions to enter dreams and stop the demons' attacks."

"You mean I would be fighting demons. I have no skill." Sean hissed, turning his neck to the right.

"You humans are an exciting lot," Alexis said with a frustrated look. "We do love you, but you can be dumb as rocks. You will be sent to go on several missions with a trained and more experienced Dreamweaver. Most Dreamweavers travel alone, depending on the type of demonic presence present. You will be given a gauge where you can read the demon's sinister nature. Eventually, you would develop a sixth sense to understand how demons operate in your physical realm. In time, you may be able to earn your way into paradise. This is not a guarantee; you can be tempted like anyone else can in the dream world. It is not for the faint of heart. Demons have the power to destroy your soul."

Sean thought of all the superhero movies he saw as a child and what type of outfit he would have. The part about dying and demons left his mind, and all he thought about was to slay them quick with whatever training he would receive.

"You seem to be awe-struck." Alexis looked at Sean with a slight smile. "Don't worry, the training won't kill you, but it'll feel like death. Demons are a fierce adversary, and we have to save as many humans as possible."

"Save humans, I mean, what will that even look like?"

"You enter dreams, and you save them. The demons die. I have nothing else to say. Samantha will guide you to your rest area, and you will start training immediately. That is all." Alexis looked down at the book in front of her using a pencil in her right hand to scribble something down.

Samantha nodded as she looked over at Sean, standing there still flabbergasted, glaring at the tiny angel. Samantha let out a short cough.

"Thank you, Alexis," Sean said in a hurried tone. "It is an honor to be here to do our best to serve in whatever capacity, don't expect much for me; I'm a feeble human. I've never helped myself in my life, and this is different for me. I am prideful."

"I like this." Alexis looked up for a moment and back at her paperwork. "Samantha, take care of him, please."

Samantha nodded as she turned quickly, and Sean followed suit. They went through a door to the right.

Sean's eyes once again felt as if he was in a daydream of sorts. The door led back to the room from before, and it seemed like he had just woken up. Looking back, he saw the door vanish as they hit the ground back in front of the cranky angel from earlier.

"I see Alexis didn't kill him or send him to The Void, so he's going to be one of those Dreamweaver's. I can see a loser from a mile away." The cranky angel shift his left shoulder a loud crack resonating around the magical room.

"I have hope in him," Samantha says. "I've watched him his whole life though I wish you would be more attentive. But if this is a chance for redemption, I'm going to make sure he's trained up with the best people we have here."

The old angel scoffed as he flew back up, opened another book, and wrote with a quill in a language Sean couldn't understand.

"When I get power, I think I'm going to take that guy on in a fight." Sean put his fist together.

Samantha walked forward, looking at Sean with a smile. "Even the weakest among us can take a novice Dreamweaver. You would do well not to challenge him. In his heyday, he was a great fencer in Paradise. None can match his strength or his speed. He struck with precision, but age does affect us all."

Sean tapped his thumbs together. "Your age. I thought angels lived forever. I believed the Goddess Anastasia made y'all infinite to be here forever to watch over us. It makes no sense to me you can die."

"Remember what I told you," Samantha said. "The way a spiritual being can be killed by someone of a similar nature. We can die because demons have the power to kill us. But we are firm in our own right, and a good goddess has given us strength to fight against the monsters, and most of all, to care for fragile humans. And she created humans from mana. Mana, is what you're going to use to draw out your power. Now that you are a spiritual body, you are connected to mana more than ever."

Sean nodded slowly. "Mana, I heard about it in church. The priest would always talk about the Goddess Anastasia and her love for us."

"You would have done well to listen more to the priest," Samantha said, walking forward from the library near the entrance location.

Samantha opens the door, once again astonished at what he saw. There were a variety of apartments and single-family homes. They weren't incredibly lavish, but they did have a particular charm about them. They looked like medieval-style homes but with modern conveniences. He looked up at what he thought was the sun. The ground beneath him was silver mixed with cobblestone. It was smooth to the touch and almost perfect in a sense.

"Divine Angel," a woman said, bowing and looking at Samantha. The woman also cut a slight smile at Sean.

Sean smiled back at the woman, trying not to blush. *Man, she was a looker.*

"Yes, there are attractive people here. But love is not your focus. I want you to know about love as part of the Dreamweaver Society. Many people get married but having children here is impossible."

"Can I have sex?" Sean put his two index fingers together, waiting for an answer.

"I guess you'll have to find out," Samantha said, walking forward. She let go a slight giggle before walking toward the corner to a small condo.

Sean looked up, and he saw the sign in front of him changed his name. *Sean Willton.* Something invisible had written his name under a small piece of wood beside the door.

"Welcome home, Sean." Samantha gleamed back at him, who was almost in tears.

Sean wiped his eyes. For the first time in his life, he felt someone cared about him. *I'm going to work hard to be worth saving.*

Chapter 2

Sean stood silent, his almond eyes taken aback by the blessing given to him. *Home? What is home? I never felt at home. I miss Tabatha.*

"Your home is a modern medieval cottage from the history of humans. We fashioned this home for you because you enjoyed fantasy novels. Some homes are similar to olden style while other homes look like they are from the 21st century."

Sean ran forward, breaking out of his awe-struck trance, yanking the front door open. "This two-bedroom one-story condo is mine. This design is my own. No one will tell me I can't have this or that."

"To an extent, yes, you can go and purchase items. This is not paradise; we do give you modest accommodations." Samantha looked at Sean, who was gazing up at her with warm eyes. "You get 5000 gold coins to shop at the mall to get whatever you need and want. There is a bank where you can save up your money. The currency is from Paradise. So, you may feel a bit woozy with euphoria when you first touch it. The gold coins are in a chest over there."

Sean was too busy looking around to a one-story home he didn't notice the giant red chess with a golden lock on it in the far-right corner. Wow. *This is like out of a movie.*

The calm angel bowed, her cotton candy hair nearly touching the floor. "I've watched you your whole life, so, I was the one who did the research. Though I'm not with you always, I am with you often. There are times where I do have to return here to check up on others. I definitely was there when you almost died when you were five years old."

"Oh yeah, my mom told me I almost drowned in the backyard pool. She told me it was a miracle I came back to life." Sean walked over to the red chest as he felt a smile come over his face.

Samantha nodded. "It was the choice of the Goddess Anastasia to bring you back to life. I was given power by her to put life back into your bones. You will continue to study and understand how mana impacts the earth and what it means to be a spiritual creature. This is not going to be easy. Salvation is going to take work."

"You know, no one ever believed in me growing up. They tolerated me. It was like I was in a dream of sorts. I often watched TV and placed myself as a character in the show. I could have a family that cared for and loved me. I guess this was maybe why I gave my parents so much hell growing up."

Samantha looked away for a moment. "You've had a long journey. I would get some rest and go shopping tomorrow. We do not operate on your concept of time here in the Dreamweaver's Society. Since we work with humans, we use standard twenty-four hours, and we replicate night to make you feel comfortable. The love of Anastasia or pure mana energy is light enough to cover all this place she created. So, night will fall, and there will be rain and all the elements you experienced when you were on Earth."

Sean started to tremble for a moment, and he put his hands on his chest. "Will I ever be able to go back?" Tears started to flow on his cheeks.

Samantha looked at Sean with twinkling eyes. *Oh dear.*

Sean wobbled a bit, his eyes lid blinking rapidly. "I feel like I'm going to throw up."

Samantha walked up to Sean and put her hand on his forehead. Without a word, Sean's body went limp, as if put into a coma.

Young one you are so much more important to me than you know Samantha thought, looking at Sean, who was passed out. *He almost threw upon himself, and then he would have gone to the doctor for spiritual healing. I'm glad I was here to help him.* She smiled as she carried his limp body over to the bed. "Rest, sweet one. You're going to need all your strength for what lies ahead." Samantha gently stroked his head. Bending down, her lips met his forehead. She cast a final glance at him before closing the front door.

Several hours later...

Sean leaped up, his heart rate elevated. *What happened? Where is Samantha?* He looked at the red chest, still there awaiting his hands to touch it. *I thought I was going to pass out.* He looked out the window the stars illuminating the night sky. The clock on the wall said 3 a.m. *My head hurts.*

Sean glanced over at the stove. The hardware was historic in nature. He saw a pot sitting there. Shifting his feet over the bed he stumbled to the counter top. He opened the cabinet and saw several flavors of tea and coffee. *Samantha did her research. They have my favorite coffee here, which is vanilla bean. They also have milk tea which I enjoyed many times with Tabatha.*

Tabatha, where is she? Sean started to feel sick again, tears flowing down his face. *Goddess, where are you? Where is my love?* Sean tried to feel happy, but he missed the love of his life. He wanted to hold her in his hands. He wanted to feel her touch... be inside her. *I guess I can't do anything about it now.*

He made his tea a little bit different from other people. He boiled the water with the teabags in it. Many people thought he was weird for this, but he found it to be the best way to pull all the flavor of the teabags.

Sean's eyes traced every detail in the room. The curtains were purple in color. There was carpet in the kitchen, and the floor was cobblestone. They look like they were made of silver and gold. He looked around, and he saw pictures of himself from when he was on Earth. He noticed Samantha behind him.

She was always there with me. I need to think. They said I have training coming up.

What am I going to fight with? Who's going to train me? Sean looked at a strange little doll. It looked like something out of a cartoon from years ago. Walking closer, he observed the wings that were red in color. Its eyes were narrow, and a smile was plastered underneath the doll's nose.

"You have a message," a female voice said.

A message at this time in the morning—they must be watching me. That thing is creepy. Sean backed up a little bit from the doll. It looked a little bit like Samantha but not real.

Sean pressed his hands on the red button on the doll's hand. A voice spoke up.

"You are to report to the Dreamweaver training facility at 7 a.m. A package will be delivered at 6:30 in the morning with everything you need. Come dressed and ready to train. Your new destiny starts now. Please remember The Void is awaiting you if you do not put in your best effort."

The Void! Where all the souls go to be tortured. I'd rather not go there.

The kettle on the stove started to steam a bit. Opening another cabinet revealed various cups, including one he had as a young child with a cat on it. He always found cats fascinating. The way they hunt and the way they could be innocent yet savage at the same time.

I guess this place isn't too bad. It's going to take some getting used to, though. Sean poured himself a cup of tea. Reaching over to the small bowl beside him, he poured the sugar into the cup, giving it a slight stir. Glancing around the room, the oversized chair made of velvet beckoned him.

I miss you, mom and dad. I miss you, Tabatha. Sean began crying; tears fell into his tea. *What the hell is this place? I'm not a fighter; I'm not a demon killer. I'm a jerk, a loser, an underachiever my whole life, and they say I must go and help people when I cannot even help myself. Does the Goddess Anastasia offer redemption and salvation? Am I even worth it? Will Samantha desert believe me?*

Sean sat there in silence, sipping his tea. *Samantha says I'm worth it. I wonder how Goddess Anastasia made the angels. They have to get made righ*t. The questions continue to race through Sean's mind as he began to drift off to sleep again.

Several hours later... again

Sean popped up when he heard three solid knocks on the door.

He wiped his eyes. "Hold on, I'm coming." As he opened the door, he saw a young woman with glasses holding a box a bit too large for her.

"Please take it," she said in a squeaky voice; her knees were beginning to buckle underneath her. I can't hold it much longer.

"Oh yeah, right," Sean said, grabbing the box. "Oh my. How do you carry this?" He put the box on the ground in front of her.

"We train for this," the young woman said as she put her feet together and gave him a firm salute. "Dreamweaver Society Postal Service is here to serve everyone. We must get packages here on time and keep the operation running. We must keep every-thing running efficiently if we're going to make it and destroy the demons. If you don't have what you need, I get yelled at. My emotions are fragile. I'm trying to get salvation as well."

Sean glared at the young woman in the long blue slacks with a white button-up shirt. She wore a blue and white hat on her head that was round with an eagle on it. *Sexy Uniform… no, I can't be thinking like that.* "Wait, so you can earn salvation as well by working in a post office?" Sean looked puzzled at the woman. She looked right back at him with her eyes widened.

"They didn't tell you." Her lips quivered ever the sightliest as if she wanted to say something, but she turned around and went back to her cheerful demeanor. "It's not my place. Everyone always told me when I got here, all will be revealed in time. Do your best, and I hope to see you around."

Sean was trying to get the words out of his mouth, but he was still in a sleepy slumber. "What's your name?"

"It's Melody," she spoke. Her long dark pigtails waived in the morning as he noticed two small dark spots on her back. "Till next time, do your best, Mr. Dreamweaver."

Sean tried to yell back his name, but the words didn't seem to leave his lips. *Right, my name is on the box. She knows my name. But there's a horrible first impression. I want to tell her so much more. I had questions. What about earning your salvation through the post office? I can't wrap my mind around all of this.*

Sean sat there looking at the heavy box. He took a deep breath. *My time is running out. I need to get to the training grounds soon. Maybe there is something in the box to give me a clue.*

Bringing the box inside, he sat on his sofa and opened it. It's a small blue book with gold writing on it. It had his name and where his destiny could change at a moment's notice.

"How poetic," Sean said, putting the notebook aside. Digging into the box, he found a gray pair of slacks that looked like a business suit, white shirt, black belt, and a long cape to wear along with it. *Looks quite fancy, especially for a date.* At the bottom of the box was a picture of how to wear the outfit. "I know how to wear a suit," Sean scoffed, putting the instruction aside.

I feel like of secret agent with this out. He was curious about the size, so he looked at the tags. He saw an S on it.

There's a small sticky note from Samantha in red. *Of course, we know your size, silly.*

Sean took a moment to laugh. Disrobing quickly, he put on the suit, which included a bright red tie. Walking in front of the mirror, he noticed how striking it looked. *Now, this is what I'm talking about. It's custom fit, too. No part of the outfit is too tight. I could never afford clothes like these on Earth. The Goddess Anastasia wants me to succeed If they're giving me this type of gear.*

Sean looked in the box saw a pair of brown gloves and brown loafers. There was a note attached. Upon completion of initial training, you will be given a weapon of choice. Your weapon will be an extension of yourself, but you will be evaluated by the head staff in the training facility. Upon a successful evaluation, the staff then will decide what would be the best weapon of choice on your journey to salvation.

Sean moved over at the clock and read 6:45 a.m. Looking back through the box to make sure there wasn't anything wrong, he heard birds chirping. Running toward the windowing opening his eyes once again gazed in awe. It looked like something out of his wildest dreams. There were towers made of gold that reached into the sky. Dragons flying to and fro. It was as if there was an interstate in the sky made of people flying.

Sean walked out the door fully dressed and looked to the left and the right for assistance.

"Hello, you," Samantha said with a smile.

Sean looked up to see his Guardian Angel who was twenty feet up above him, flying in a circle.

Descending from the sky like a dove, her feet gently touched the ground. "Like I said, I'm not going to let you fail. I will show you how to get there. The rest will be up to you."

Sean nodded, stepping back at the beauty of Samantha. "Good morning, and thank you."

"Now, I want you to close your eyes and lean forward as if you were going to fall flat on your stomach," Samantha said.

"Why would I do that?" Sean mused.

"Do it." Samantha grunted. You're going to be late."

Sean closed his eyes and mumbled, "You'd better be right."

"Here we go," Samantha said as she smiled, walking behind him. She caught Sean right before he fell to the ground, raising him up into the air.

Sean saw the ground beneath them disappear. "Oh my gosh, oh my gosh. We're gonna die, I'm gonna die!"

"You're already dead, remember?" They appeared to be in full stride. Samantha giggled, holding him in her arms. "You would resist. Plus, you trust me, don't you? I've always been there for you, so there's no way I would let you die. It's a lot of fun to see you squirm," Samantha said, laughing loud as she took a sharp right turn in the air.

"I get it, I get it." He was upset now. "I can't even have a chance to take in all the beautiful sights," Sean yelled. He saw a giant pool of water with a waterfall underneath. "Will we be able to visit the waterfall one of these days?" *The scenery reminds me of a tropical vacation.*

Samantha said, "Anything you experience here in a Dreamweaver's Society will be ten times better than what Earth had to offer. I guess one day you'll be able to visit. Right now, focus on your training."

The moment Sean stared back, he felt his body once again go to an intense freefall with the angel. As the ground narrowed closer, he closed his eyes the wind rushing across his cheeks.

Chapter 3

Sean ogled the massive structure, which was covered in gold bricks. His eyes traced the different paintings on the windows. All he knew was that they were beautiful, and he was thankful to have his feet on the ground.

The sliding doors open as a man runs out. "You can't make me do it; you can't make me do it; I don't want to." He ran up toward Sean and grabbed him by the arm.

"Dont let them take me back in there." The man's eyes were red like fire. His hands were sweaty, hanging onto Sean for dear life.

Samantha tapped Sean on the shoulder twice. Don't say a word. "That is Saul, the tall, muscular man in a black trench coat with a hood on walking towards you."

Without a word, the man in the trench coat snatches the scared skinny man and drags him back to the building.

"What was that?" Sean scurried toward Samantha, looking up at her with curiosity in his eyes.

"The one whom was clinging from you rejected the proposal of becoming a Dreamweaver." Samantha looked at him, and she proceeded forward.

Sean followed Samantha through the doors. He saw a cheerful young man in a business suit sitting at work at the check-in area.

Samantha walked forward as the man smiled and looked at Sean, and nodded.

"This way," Samantha stated, winking at Sean. They walked through a series of passageways that were painted blue and pink. It felt like walking through a hallway of cotton candy. The color resembled Sean's favorite football team when he was younger.

He almost bumped into Samantha, who looked back at him.

"Whatever happens, don't give up," Samantha said. She extended her arm, pulling him close, her lips pressing against Sean's sweaty forehead.

Sean gazed at her. He felt like a frog was stuck in his throat. *I'm terrified.*

Proceeding through the doors, he noticed a large room with several different people of different sizes shooting objects. Some were in outfits like his, while others were in skimpier attire. It reminded him of the battle shows he watched as a child.

Sean walked over to the counter with Samantha. He looked at the man who was standing in front of a tall bookcase.

"Intro training," the man said to Samantha with a smile. "There seem to be a lot of people who are transitioning through here lately. I guess the dead are indeed coming in at a rapid rate." The man presses the button. "You guys are in room one. They're already waiting for you."

"They?" Sean acknowledged sheepishly. His mouth was a dry as a desert. His right foot tapped the floor as if counting the rhythm of a song.

The duo rounded the corner from the desk. It was a two-minute walk to the room they were supposed to be in. The one-way glass sliding doors opened as Sean and Samantha stepped forward.

"It's about time you showed up." A stern man with a trim beard and charcoal skin sneered at Sean.

Samantha bowed gracefully toward the man. "We were running a little bit behind. I'll be taking a seat over here and watch and wait to see what happens."

"All right, chump." The muscular man crossed his arms, his upper lip quivering.

Sean glanced around the room. He took his thumb and pointed it toward himself. "Me, a chump!?"

"That's right," the man bellowed, "you are a chump. It's my job to make sure you don't die out there on your first mission. You have no fighting ability at all. You suck at fighting. You take one step into the dream realm, and you will die a horrible spiritual death. Demons don't play around."

Sean smacked his cheeks twice, shaking his head, trying to wipe the fear off his face. "My name is Sean." His eyes surveyed the muscular dark skin man with all the faith he could muster in his heart. The man reminded him of the bouncers he used to see at the club.

The man looked at Sean up with his eyebrow raised. "I'm not your friend, and you will have to earn my respect. You can call me Macedon."

Sean nodded, his impassioned eyes glaring at Macedon.

Sean saunters up to Macedon. His breath hastened with each step. The thoughts in his mind raced like hamsters in a maze.

Macedon bent his head down, leaning down toward Sean, his chin almost touching Sean's head. He put his massive hands on the recruits shoulders. "Yes, yes, I see," he uttered.

Sean didn't know what to think. He thought about the massive hands and Macedon towering over his body. He could be crushed at a moment's notice.

Macedon turned around and went toward the wall and knocked on it twice. A table flipped over from the wall showing a variety of weapons from polearms, wands, and swords. "Come on over here," the dark skin man said, looking at Sean.

Sean walked over to look at the weapons. This was a great time to see which one would best fit him. It would be the weapon he would take with him on missions if he could even get past training. *Macedon seems to look forward to punishing me. What do I pick?*

"Don't make me wait all day," Macedon declared, walking away. "Pick a weapon and let me observe it."

Sean looked. He noticed a long pole with a dragon on it. *It looks like my sort of weapon.* Touching it, he sees his initials form at the hilt. *That is too cool!*

Sean walked over to Macedon, gripping the pole, his hand trembling.

"Now, try to hit me," Macedon bellowed.

"All right, here I come," Sean said. He arched his foot back as he ran forward, slamming the pole toward Mastodon's neck. *Where did he go?* There was nothing but empty space in front of him.

"How pathetic," Macedon gloated. "How can you even call that a strike? My job is to make certain your strength to focus on your physical stamina. You'll go through several challenges today. First will be your physical stamina, next will be your mental stamina, and last will be your spiritual energy. All this training makes a Dreamweaver effective in the spiritual realm. Without being able to understand each essential component, you will die."

Does he mean die and go into The Void? Sean looked up to see Macedon right in front of him. Shifting to the left, Sean leaped forward, slamming the pole on Macedon's shoulder.

Macedon took his pinky finger and lightly pushed the pole off his shoulder with ease. "Put the weapon down, boy. You're not even fit to hold it yet. Samantha, what do you see in this clown? Can he be a Dreamweaver? You'll be better off in the post office or where they deliver food."

Samantha glanced over at Macedon with a smile. "I have faith in him. All oak trees start as a seed."

The kind words of Samantha warmed his heart. *How can she be confident in me?* His best was akin to most individuals' mediocre.

"All right, shrimp, first squats, watch me. We're going to build up your little legs so you can increase your stamina." The large man bent toward the ground and back up. He went up and down forty-five times.

"Now join me, let's go now," Macedon yelled, "squat one, two, three, four, five."

"Yes, yes," Sean said. He bent down quickly, not even realizing how it would go, "one, two, three, four, five, six, seven, eight, nine, ten." He repeated the squats. Reaching forty, Sean's legs buckled, sweat pouring over his body.

"Good," Macedon said, "you didn't die in the first set of forty. We have two more sets of forty to go. Let's get it in!"

Sean squatted again, his heart beating a thousand times a minute. *They made me do this; they made me feel like this. What are they thinking? I feel like my body is a pool of sweat.* The ground seemed closer than usual as he lifted his head, looking up at Macedon. His neck felt as if it weighed four times its size. He went to squat again to try to get to forty; he was exhausted. He fell on his back, breathing heavily. "Why am I not in workout clothes?"

"You are training for real-life scenarios. If you were in gym clothes, you wouldn't be able to train well." Macedon leaning over a smile plastered on his face. "You will experience all sorts of elements in the spiritual realm. Don't worry, you will get a new suit."

Samantha looked at Sean, giving him a thumbs-up. "This is only the start of the day. We have so much more we have to go through."

I don't know if I can take anymore. I hated to work out in the real world, and now I must work out in the spiritual world. His muscles ached. *What happened to this being a perfect body or a better body?*

Macedon looked at Sean, his like steaming like volcano. "If you don't train your spiritual body, then you won't be any good to anybody. It's not like you're in paradise, where you get your perfect body. Here you got to work for it. It is the same rules on Earth. Food, sleep, and everything is essential for your growth here. There are slight differences, and you'll figure them out along the way. Any who, I can't keep you here anymore. Samantha is going to take you to the next step of training. I expect to see you here tomorrow morning, ready to grind it out more."

Sean wanted to punch Macedon in the face, but he knew better than to challenge the muscle-bound freak. "Thank you for the help." He bowed, never taking his eyes off his trainer.

Macedon huffed, lowering his neck, slowly acknowledging Sean, offering, "You're going to need a lot more than help to survive out there, kid."

Samantha leaped up as she walked over to Sean, putting her hand on his shoulder. "Don't worry, you'll make it, now onto the next part of training."

The angel took a right outside the door going to another hallway which was littered with images of cats and dogs in suits.

Sean observed the photos, the sweat taking time to dry on his skin. The pictures reminded him of the viral videos he used to watch."Where are we going?" Sean asked.

"The person you're going to meet is good-hearted but a bit different." Samantha opened the door, and he walked into a small circular sphere of sorts. There was a woman standing there talking to herself. She giggled out loud at Samantha and Sean.

A female voice piped up. "Warrior Angel, you are here with another victim… I mean person. I can't help myself; I am ready to torture this poor soul. He doesn't even know what's about to happen."

Sean wanted to turn around, but the door behind him magically disappeared. He huddled closer to Samantha. The terror swelled over his body. *Who or what in the world is she?*

"This is Emery," Samantha says. "She is, I would say, a test of your mental fitness."

"Yes, my tests are the hardest, and I do my research to make sure the questions in my exams will put your mind in a tizzy. I will not push you but help you become the best Dreamweaver possible." The chubby angel twirled in circles forty-five times. She jumped up into the air and slammed her hand on the desk. "I don't mess around. This shit is about to get real."

"I didn't know angels cussed," Sean said. *She's going to kill my brain, if I even have one left. Do I even have a brain? That balance its other worldly.*

Samantha didn't seem bothered with the antics. She went over to the small couch on the left-hand side and told Sean to step up to the desk.

"Can I at least get something to drink?" Sean said.

"Do you think all of this happens by accident? You should be in The Void right now, a person like you. Selfish, trying to put on a good front. I am wasting my time with you. I do what the Goddess Alexis tells me to. We are short on Dreamweaver's, and even if you aren't quality, I will make you sufficient. Take a seat," Emery said. She snapped her fingers, tilting her head to the right winking mischievously.

Before Sean could walk forward, he felt his butt land in a soft chair. The chair sped forward. At the same time, a strap came over his lap, strapping him into the seat.

"You have two hours to finish this test." Her pink and black dress flowed around her. She was thrilled and skipped around Sean, who couldn't move at all.

"Relax, Sean, I'm here, nothing can happen to you," Samantha said.

"Are you sure about that!?" Sean looked over, his eyes wide at his Guardian Angel. "I feel like I'm about to die. I'm good, man, I'm good. Get me out of his chair. Send me to The Void."

Emery stopped looking over at Sean, her blue eyes fierce as the ocean's waves. "Don't you dare say those words," she said. "It is by the grace of Anastasia you are sitting in this seat. You were destined for The Void, and Samantha vouched for you. She spoke of your mediocre good deeds in front of the council."

Sean sat there, his eyes surveying Samantha. *What did she do?* He was lost in his thoughts until he felt Emery pat him on the shoulder.

Emery leaned in close to Sean's ear. "She can tell you the rest when she's ready. Now it's time for your test." The plump angel then put a small cup in front of her and poured coffee. She mixed in two creamers and three sugars. "There you go," she said putting the brown cup in front of Sean. "You have two hours."

Sean gripped his pen; his mind raced as he looked at the first question. His mouth dropped in awe.

Chapter 4

Sean's eyes didn't move. The question in front of him foretold immense destruction. *What are they thinking? If I answer this wrong, I'm going to go into The Void either way.* Sean sat there, wondering if this was cruel and unusual punishment. The question read, *"Do you think your Guardian Angel is sexy?"*

The legit question had the number one next to it. *Think, Sean. Think, what do I do, what do I do?* He did what every man would do and pushed the button.

Sean clenched his teeth. He thought he was going to be dropped into some sort of bottomless pit and go to the depths of the hallway to be tortured forever. To his surprise, he saw the test click over to number two. He knew he was in the clear. He tried not to smile. *How can I not find my Guardian Angel sexy? She is seven feet tall with a 14-foot wing span and carries a sword which can slice anything in half.*

I can do this. Sean looked at the next question. *If you could go back in time and assassinate a world leader as a child, would you do it?*

Sean wasn't ready for this type of vigorous test. He could feel his palms sweating. *They are going to kill me if I would kill it, the baby. I could never kill a child. I mean, I will destroy the adult version of the person, but I would not kill an innocent baby. Maybe I would kill the parents.* He saw two bubbles on the computer screen, yes or no. *Couldn't they give me a paragraph option? I could explain my thought process.*

Sean sat there for a minute. He glanced over at Emery, who danced in a circle taunting Samantha with a silly gesture.

The next two hours of the psychological exam got worse with no end in sight.

Sean noticed one question which referenced the order of the chicken or the egg. *Why would they phrase it like that? I always hated that question.*

Sean clicked no because he had no idea what it meant. *Maybe it was a joke question.* Sean looked over at the clock, and he had ten minutes left.

He clicked over to the next question, and it stunned him as much as the first. *Do you believe the Goddess Anastasia can bring people back from The Void?*

Sean sat there and thought of all the lessons he heard of the goddess and her grace and mercy. He thought maybe the Goddess Anastasia created The Void. She had all the power to do with it as she pleases. *If she is all powerful, I see no reason why she couldn't bring someone back.*

Sean clicks the yes button as he was suddenly hit in the face with an array of confetti spray out of a contraption from the desk.

"Congratulations," Emery joyfully yelled, and she jumped up into the air in front of Samantha as she landed beside him and clicked the button underneath the chair. "You're free to go now," she cheered. "Results will be given to you soon."

"Can't I know now?" Sean said, looking at the chubby angel with questioning eyes.

"No, you cannot, now leave. You would ruin all the fun. Samantha, help him to move along now. He needs to get to his final test of the day."

Samantha looked slightly annoyed; she had listened to Emery blab on for two hours. Sean did not hear any of it, though, because it seemed as if there was a barrier around him to keep the noise out. Though he could tell by her facial expressions every now and then when he was looking over at her that she wasn't having fun.

Sean stood up and walked over to Samantha, his hand shaking uncontrollably. "My blood sugar is low if that is a thing that happens here," Sean groaned.

Samantha nodded, putting her hands together gently. "It's noon your time, as far as humans are concerned. We should go get lunch."

Those sweet words danced around Sean's ears. He hadn't eaten anything since he arrived for training.

Walking to the other side of the room, Samantha opened the door with Sean trailing behind. He saw they were led to a sort of escalator. Sean looked over to the right, and he saw ads representing different foods for the food court they were headed to.

"Are you okay, Sean?" Samantha inquired. "You appear flustered. What did Emery talk to you about?" Samantha looked back at him as she was quickly walking the stairs.

"You wouldn't understand," he mumbled.

"There are certain things humans can't comprehend about our realm. I can try to explain it to but you would have to spend a lifetime in the library of enchantment. We are complex beings, and I try my best to relate to you. But I'm okay if you don't tell me. We're going to get your favorite meal. And then, after a moment of rest, you will go to your next test, and then you will speak to the council."

Sean looked at a checkpoint when they came up to the food court. It looked like a sort of giant dryer. Samantha walked around it as she pointed toward this contraption Sean had to walk through. They looked like big fans, and when he looked, he was scared.

"What is this?" Sean asked Samantha, "and what is it going to do to me?" Sean saw Samantha's face and knew she was hungry, so he walked toward the machine.

He closed his eyes, and smelt something reminiscent to the spring showers from Earth, and his clothes magically dry from all the sweat and perspiration from before. It felt like euphoria. This feeling soon stopped, and he walked out fresh and clean.

"What was that?" Sean asked.

Samantha put her hand out, beckoning him toward her. "That machine uses your mana to refresh your soul. It's a very intense contraction. It's spiritually powered by the individual who walks through. So, depending on your mana, you may restore a bit or you may not refresh at all. It means you weren't too tired from your test today, so that's a good thing. In essence, it was spiritual deodorant for your semi-physical body. It dried your sweat and cleaned the funk off you."

Sean nodded his head. He understood what the tall angel stated. They rounded the corner and the food court came into view. He was curious what the cuisine was like in this Dreamweaver Society. People of all colors and sizes walked briskly across the massive dining area.

"Can I ask you something?" Sean looked up at Samantha, who was walking gracefully beside him with her hands folded over one another.

"Of course, what's on your mind?' Samantha had a bit of concern in her soul but kept it at bay as she looked over at Sean.

"Why was I picked to be a Dreamweaver? It would appear everyone here has a job like Earth and depending on the job, it seems you could do anything to work your way into paradise. Is there a time limit or time constraints compared to Earth years? I'm curious."

Samantha took a deep sigh, and as she was about to open her mouth, a young woman ran up to Sean.

"Hey, do you remember me?" the shy but cheerful woman asked.

Sean thought back to their encounter. "Yes, I do. You're Melody," he answered.

41

Melody stood at five foot ten, her big circular glasses covered most of her face, and she carried a sincere smile. Often, she looks like a nervous wreck. Her knees buckled a lot, which was from carrying so many packages.

"A friend of yours?" Samantha gushed, interested in the woman.

"Yeah, we met once." Sean felt a tug on his right hand.

Melody grabbed his hand and pulled him toward the food court. "We're going to be the best of friends. You're the first person who treated me with respect. The Postal Service is the lowest job you can get in the spiritual realm, remember," she said.

"Really, no one treats you nice." Sean was still trying to steady his feet which were almost off the ground. *She's got a strong grip for her size. It could be all of those packages she delivers.*

Melody stopped abruptly, Sean almost slamming into her back. "You don't get a choice. No, this is what we're going to eat today."

Sean looked up, and he saw a hibachi place of sorts. "I do love a good hibachi. I could go for some clams and rice." Sean grinned.

Melody's legs went up and down as if doing leg lifts. "My treat, this is the Monday when I get paid."

"Paid?" Sean said.

"Yeah, didn't you read the handbook?" She jumped close to Sean, her glasses almost leaping off her face. "It's supposed to explain everything out for you. It shows you how you get money currency, your spiritual card. You should be getting one in the mail. They pay with gold, it's a gold card, and it's kind of like a credit card, and the hours you work exchange into currency. So, since you haven't worked in the hours, you probably don't have money. They start you off with one hundred gold."

She seems shy, but not really. What have I gotten myself into? Sure, she was cute. Sean did like a woman who took charge. Her personality reminded him of his beloved Tabatha.

Sean was looking at the impressive decor outside the restaurant when a man stepped forward, looking at Melody and Sean.

"The regular," the man said, beaming at Melody.

"Yep, always," she responded to the cheerful man. She looked back at Sean and smiled at him.

Melody twirled in a circle. "This is my special day. It's fun and fancy Monday. I took half a day off today. This place has the best hibachi in all of the food court."

Sean noticed the pillars silver in color, and different booths had brown seats and tables. Each had its own personal grill master and private sections. They were also sections that had large group meets and people who were at the bar having a quick drink. The ceiling was extravagant with swords floating magically twirling around each other. People were dressed in suits like him, and he thought they could be fellow Dreamweaver's in training.

Sean walked through two double doors with Melody, and they came to a separate booth with four seats.

"Thank you for joining me," Melody said, "and I'll get the usual," she told a chef.

Sean took a seat, not really knowing what to say. He heard classical music full of cellos and violins. There was a slight hint of a guitar over the speakers above him.

A few moments later, Samantha showed up, looking at Sean with a slight smile.

Sean didn't know what to think. All he knew was this cheerful woman took them back into a private bar for hibachi.

Samantha took a seat next to Sean. She nodded at him and put her hands gracefully on the table. "Before you steal my young man here, may be a little bit overwhelmed."

Overwhelmed was an understatement. Sean sat there and tried to look at the menu. His stress started to fade as he noticed that the food was familiar. It was shrimp and clam hibachi with spicy sauce. Sweet tea to top off what his taste buds were yearning for.

"How much does this cost you?" Sean asked the energetic postal worker.

44

"About half a month's work." Melody's cheeks perked up, looking at the menu, already knowing what she wanted but waiting to let Sean figure it out.

A half of a month, what, for hibachi? Sean couldn't comprehend the currency exchange for work. Hibachi back home had cost $15, but here it was so much more.

"She spends way too much money on this stuff." A man grunted.

Melody turned around and smiled big. "Maximus, you were able to make it."

Sean gaped at the slender yet toned angel dressed in all white with a red bow tie adorning his neck. His complexion was dark as night.

"Why do you want me to join you in such trivial things?" Maximus bleated.

"Hi, Maximus," Samantha said, looking at him with cheerful eyes.

"Still keeping humans as pets," he said to Samantha his anthracite eyes cutting a glance at Sean. Maximus looked over at a waiter who was nearby and pointed two fingers signaling him to come over to where he was. "If you could be so kind, could you bring me a red wine with strawberries in it, please?"

The man nodded. "Is everyone ready to order?" the man asked.

Sean was curious if everyone who was working here had some sort of identification on their outfit but didn't notice any. He popped up, saying, "Can I get the hibachi shrimp and clams? Slightly spicy, please."

Samantha looked at Sean with a smile. "I would like the white rice and lobster hibachi mild, please."

"And I will take the super spicy hibachi clams, shrimp, and lobster," Melody said with a smile.

Maximus scoffed for a moment, and then with a slight smile, he looked at the cheerful young woman. "You do know you should use your currency to maybe save up for better living arrangements."

"You know Maximus, I want to have a little bit of fun," Melody crooned. She sat there and focused on the dark angel who had his arms crossed and his eyes slightly closed.

"Do what you will," Maximus said. "Boy, do you know what Samantha has done for you?" he inquired as he took a sip of wine.

Sean felt an aura of arrogance he remembered from the church from his adolescent years. Many people who worshipped Anastasia were full of themselves, and he hated them. He wanted nothing to do with their religious cult or their ability to bless people. *I could probably knock him out in a matter of five seconds or less.*

Sean took a deep breath. "I mean, I know angels protect me. I know Samantha looked out for me, and maybe they were divine circumstances of protection."

"Have you read all of the rulebooks? If you're going to be a Dreamweaver, you need to act like one and have elegance and dignity. You are going to be above most of the people who work in our society. Most of the humankind here support Dreamweaver's because it is the most dangerous job to pursue to your path to paradise." Maximus said to Sean with a cunning tone.

Sean wanted to be out of sight. He felt like he was being talked to like a child. *I don't need a lecture on the philosophical nature of the spiritual realm.* His heart ached for Tabatha. *Samantha is a rarity among the angels I have met thus far.*

"What do you think I'm doing here? I am here trying to get to paradise, and I have so many things that I want to accomplish. I'm working hard," Sean said.

Maximus looked over at Samantha, who was taking a sip of water. She looked back over at him and shook her head, then looked to Sean and Melody, who were sitting there moving along to the song played on the speakers above.

Maximus let out a grunt and looked back at Sean. "Do try not to upset Samantha or those who empower you. They have faith unlike me. But if I were you, I wouldn't dare become a Dreamweaver. You don't have it in you. I'm surprised Macedon didn't tell you."

Sean got back to the massive dark skin man with muscles. *He comes to realize Maximus wasn't an angel but probably was a Dreamweaver himself. Maybe that is why he was so helpful. I wonder if anyone here actually cares about anybody? What was the hi-*

erarchy of the society? Sean didn't know what to think of it, but he didn't want to cause a stink and tried to change the subject.

Sean looked over at the eccentric postal worker. "What is your favorite part about being in the Dreamweaver's Society?"

"My favorite part about being here. I guess I should start with how long I've been here. In human years, it's been about a year and a half. The time is so different here they make it relatable to us. It doesn't feel like an eternity." She twirled her thumbs, the words becoming softer as she spoke.

"Do they give you a sentence of sorts?" Sean looked curious at the petite young woman.

"Sean," The voice came from across the table. Samantha looked at him, and her eyes told him not to press forward. "Those sorts of questions are personal, and you really shouldn't ask them." Samantha hissed, clenching her teeth at Sean. "There are so many things you don't understand about where you are. But I will guide you. You should apologize."

Sean noticed Samantha's eyes and saw she wasn't joking. "Sorry, Melody, I didn't know it was such a sensitive topic."

"It's okay. It's the official rule in the rulebook. People here have lived very hard lives, but others committed such atrocities but had a change of heart when they died. You'll see," Melody said.

A man came out with a cart and with glass plates, white in color with beautiful dishes on them. Sean noticed the dish his ordered. His lips started to moisten with saliva. *There are such delica-*

cies in semi-heaven. My body needs healing after all of the torture from this morning.

"Also, you should know," Maximus bleated. "Since you're new here, Sean, your first gourmet meal is free. Places like this are a bit more expensive. You better enjoy this complimentary meal," he said.

"This is delicious," Sean yammered. The people around him looked at Sean, who was starting to cut up the shrimp and rice and put it into this mouth.

"Right," Melody replied, it's fantastic. You can see why I save up half a month's salary for it." Her mouth was full, trying to communicate to Sean.

I must work harder. Samantha is counting on me. Maximus's cold eyes were on Melody. *I wonder if he cares about her.* Sean took another bite, gulping down a fork full of shrimp and rice.

Melody looked over at Sean her cheeks flared. "I'm so glad you joined me. It's good to have someone to eat with. I don't have a lot of friends because I'm at the bottom of the totem pole. Not a lot of people wanna eat with a postal worker."

"They see you as less than," Sean speculated.

"You have yet to learn the ways of the hierarchy here in our society, Sean." Samantha crossed her arms and looked over at Melody. "Dreamweaver's sit at the top of the chain right underneath angels."

"I know." Sean looked like he was proud of himself.

"There are ways to work yourself up," Maximus said. "But it takes hard work. What you desire will come with time." If you understand the truth of what sacrifice means; maybe, you can reach paradise.

Sean felt like the slender angel spoke in riddles. "How do I get there? What do I do to get to the top? I'm sure there is a hierarchy among Dreamweaver's."

Samantha said, "yes, it's a long road."   As Maximus said, "what you put in is what you get out. You must want it. You have to want to be in paradise and put your mind to it and then nothing will stop you."

"Do people stay here for a long time? I mean, do people actually get there, or is paradise a pipedream?" Sean put his fork down and bit his upper lip. There was sense of confusion over his spirit.

"You can make it," Samantha promised. "Paradise is beautiful. It's where we come from. Many of us are on rotation and others are permanent wanting to help humans go to their final home. The Goddess Anastasia loves you and wants the best for you. But your free will at times gets in your way. Therefore, we are here, to guide you." Samantha smiled warmly both at Melody and Sean.

Maximus shook his head adverting his eyes from Melody. "I'm not emotional like my cohort here. But yes, if the Goddess Anastasia will say it is my duty to help humans get to paradise I will do so. Paradise is for those who are pure of heart and know the will of the goddess."

The group finishes up their meal and drinks their water and wine.

"Man, I am stuffed," Sean says. He looks over at Melody, who had a satisfied smile on her face looking down at her plate.

The group stood up from the table and pushed in their chairs.

"Oh, that was so good. Oh my gosh, I could sleep for ages right now. My day off was such a blessing, thank the goddess," she said, holding up her wine glass. "I am ready, I am prepared for whatever comes. Nothing can stop me!" Melody swayed back and forth as she ran toward Sean and pressed her lips on his right cheek.

Sean blushed for a moment. He didn't know how to react. *That was warm.*

"Oh dear, looks like I'm going to have to carry this one back to her house." Maximus took one sip of his red wine, placing it on the table. He bowed at Samantha.

Sean watched the tall, slenderangel scoop Melody in his arms and walked out away from the private area.

"Don't forget, Sean, go for it. You got it, man. You can do it. Nobody can stop-you, aim for your truth, and I'll be right behind you," she said in a drunken stupor leaning out of the arms of Maximus.

Sean giggled, eyeing Samantha, who was staring off in the distance at the wall."You okay?" he inquired.

"Yeah, it's nothing. I'm thinking about your subsequent trial. Your food should be digested now, and we will be head to your final training of today, which is the spiritual trial." Samantha put out her fist as Sean gave her a fist bump back.

Sean closed his eyes, a sincere smile gracing his face. Deep in his heart, he knew something was off.

Chapter 5

The pair departed from the restaurant, trying to pay for their meal but found it was ironically taken care of by Maximus.

"I guess that coldhearted angel does have a soul," Sean joked around.

"Maximum is rough around the edges, as you can see, and a bit arrogant. He tolerates me. Most angels hate him because he brings out the problems with our society etc. etc. etc." Samantha walked in front guiding him out of the food court and toward a long back hallway.

Sean looked at the door, but it didn't look like anything out of the ordinary. "Is this where we're going next for my final test?" The door above him had a sign that was lit with the word 'Cinema' on it. "Is watching a movie and trying not to cry the final test? Do I need to sit through a crappy romantic film about a man in love with a woman and maybe getting shot trying to save her?"

Samantha giggled, pressing the button on the right side of the door revealing an elevator.

"All right, let's get to it." Sean stepped through into the elevator. he immediately felt the floor beneath him disappear. "What the hell is going on?" he yelled.

Oh my gosh, oh my gosh. Sean felt like he was falling forever. There were lights on the left and the right of him twirling in different colors, like a rainbow. *I want to go back home! I want to go back to Earth. I must marry Tabatha!*

Sean wondered where Samantha was or if this was all a setup. *I can't die. I can't die.* Sean took a moment to focus as he felt his body starting to slow down. The floor beneath him was black in color with white polka dots, and he was one inch from hitting it. Breathing heavily, he took a moment to think about what happened before he hit the ground.

"So, you do have spiritual power," a voice stated from the shadows.

"Who are you?" Sean adverted his eyes to the brilliant light filled the room and a man in a lab coat with tiny glasses and a white suit. He had a stern but pleasant demeanor, and he glared at Sean as if he was a test subject of sorts.

"My name is Elijah, and I will be hosting your spiritual test today."

Sean felt his stomach hit the ground. "Ugh!" He grabbed his stomach, sitting up from the ground. "Where is Samantha? Is she coming? I can't do this without her. I need her. She is my biggest supporter here."

"Samantha is tied up in another manner, so you will be taking this test on your own. This will be the toughest test of the three. If you do not pass this one and then you have no hope of becoming a Dreamweaver."

Sean knew the way to get back to Tabatha or even have hope of getting back to her was to pass this test.

Sean steps forward from the hallway into the main area. He saw several spheres of white and blue floating around the room as if controlled by Elijah himself.

"Now, if you will, we're going to go to the door right here." Elijah walked up to another door on the side of the room.

So many doors. He must have door fetish. Sean followed Elijah closely, trying not to get lost in the maze of doors.

"I like to call these spiritual gymnastics," Elijah said with a smirk. "You stopped yourself from hitting the ground. Subconsciously, you decided you did not want to die, and your body kicked into high gear, and you were able to manifest your spiritual energy to slow your body before it hit the ground.

"Yeah, I did. It was great," Sean looked at the room. There were mini contraptions including, a slide, pull-up bar, and a human dummy in the center of the room.

"My job and my pleasure here is to help you improve your skills or draw them out of you." Elijah nodded, a fixed gaze planted on his face. "You have your work cut out for you."

Sean nodded but felt like he was being judged.

"First, what you did was slow time. Spiritual arts are extremely difficult to manifest. The art of manifesting mana takes physical and mental precision. There are Dreamweaver's who walk in arrogance overestimating their abilities and end up getting killed in the spiritual realm. Those individuals are sent into The Void because they did not know the Goddess Anastasia."

Elijah looked at Sean with curiosity, and he pointed toward a staircase. "Your first exercise will be to fall off the stairs, and I will demonstrate to you what you are supposed to do."

Sean looked at the four steps that manifested out of thin air.

Elijah walked up the steps. He put his arms out. Turning around, he fell off the fourth step.

To Sean's bewilderment, the angel stopped himself right before he hit the ground.

"You're an angel, and I'm human," Sean said, "you are leagues above me in character, stature, intellect, and wisdom. You don't even have to try."

Elijah lifted himself, landing gracefully in front of Sean. "It is precisely the fear of death you can use to push your abilities. A steady dose of fear is essential, especially when it comes to training."

"This will be good," Sean muttered rolling his hazel eyes to the left.

"Please know I'm not going to let you get hurt, at least not too much. Now it's your turn." Elijah smiled, putting his hand out to motion Sean toward the four steps.

Well, Anastasia, I hope you don't let me bust my head open. Sean took one, two, three, four steps up.

Elijah glared at Sean, his cheeks a scarlet red.

Turning around, Sean noticed the break room with equipment, and he closed his eyes. *Here we go. I hope I don't die.* Sean put his arms turning around and stepped off the stairs. *Damn!* He felt his body slam hard on the ground. Rolling on his stomach, he huffed, trying to catch his breath. "Why didn't you catch me?" Sean roared.

The witty angel clapped his hands together. "No! Did you even concentrate? Think of what makes you scared or a person you want to protect. How does the mana feel when it flows through your body? In doing so, if you're able to slow your blood flow in your heartbeat into a stream of consciousness. It is essential you master this to survive in a spiritual realm."

"Controlling my mana flow, dude; you sound like some sort of guru. But I get it, I get it. I must concentrate and if I want to reach salvation and get to my beloved Tabatha. This is what I have to do."

Elijah left eyebrow raised. "Oh, your loved one," he inquired.

"Yeah, I was going to propose to her," Sean said as he walked back around to the steps glancing at Elijah again, standing there with the same cheeky look. *I miss her smile, smell, and touch.* "I want to protect her!" Sean turned around and crossed his arms. *This is the hardest thing I've ever done.* Smack. He hit the ground hard again. "What the hell is going on? At this rate, I'm going to break my neck in half."

"Remember, you are in a spiritual body. You're slightly more substantial, which means you have stronger bones, and your mana is a stream of energy waiting to be channeled. So, you can take a few injuries to the back of the neck and not worry about it, nor would you need a chiropractor. If you want one, there are spiritual massage therapists up here, now let's get to it."

This is the worst! I would rather have a thousand scorpions on my chest. Sean storms back over to the four steps. Smack, he hit the ground again. Smack!

For the next ten minutes, Sean continued to fall on his back. Smack, smack, and smack.

"Are you harnessing your mana?" Elijah crossed his arms, glaring at the human lying on the ground. "Your outfit is stunning, I'm not going to lie, but you need to focus."

Sean lifted him self-up slower than usual. He felt the pain in his back swell. Clenching his teeth, he brushed the dust off his suit. "Well, Mr. Fancy Pants, why don't you show me again how to focus? And all the stuff about mana. I thought about Tabatha while falling. I had sex with Tabatha, I thought about hugging her, and embracing her hand."

"Who is Tabatha?" Elijah gazed intently into Sean's eyes.

Sean stood there, crossing his arms. He looked at the ground. *Who is Tabatha?* I've been thinking all about her physical nature, but what about her soul, he thought. Tabatha is kind. She wants to help dogs cross the street, and Tabatha took care of her mother when she had a heart attack. She's a nurse, so she naturally helps people.

"Sounds good, and she was a trusting person who cared for all those around her." Elijah piqued his interest.

Sean clenched his fist, his eyes glistening. "Yes, she trusted me, and we were to be married before I died tragically. I still don't know how it happened, and it bothers me. It's not like I'm going back to Earth. My goal now is to get to salvation or maybe find her in a dream here. I miss her."

Elijah took his index finger and traced it across his chin. "Humans can be so physically focused they can be of no spiritual good to themselves. Many of you walk around depressed, sad, anxious, and wait for your life to end instead of going out there and achieving greatness."

Sean's eyes locked on the steadfast angel feeling the courage swell within him. "I think I understand." Walking back up to the stairs, Sean didn't close his eyes. Sweat pouring off his arms, he screamed, "Tabatha, I love you!" Falling forward, the emotions swelled up in his body. He thought he felt the mana flow from his head to his toes.

Before Sean hit the ground, he felt his body become light and float slowly toward the ground. He looked the floor, and his nose was one inch off the hard floor. "Yeah, I did it, I did it." His focus left him the familiar ground greeting him again. "Ouch."

"You did it." Elijah chuckled as he pulled out a cloth and gave it to Sean to wipe the blood off his nose. "Well done, that was amazing. Now you can see what being a spiritual body is all about. You must put away your selfishness from the past and look inward. From what Samantha told me, you were selfish and lacked initiative on Earth."

"Yeah, you can say that." Sean stood up. Taking the tissue, he wiped his nose. "Well, I'm glad I was able to at least float a little bit." Throwing the tissue on the ground, he stepped forward, putting his right hand on Elijah's shoulder. Does it mean we can move on?"

"Quite unsatisfactory," Elijah hissed underneath his breath. "Indeed, it does, but please know this is a bare minimum of what you are capable of." The experienced angel tilted his head toward the tissue on the ground. Letting go a slight cough he pointed at the blooded ball of cloth.

"Oh!" Sean clenched his teeth, turning around, grasping the tissue dropping it into the waste basket. *I've got to do better!*

Elijah clapped his hand three times as a smile danced on his face. "We will continue to train, and you will also be able to train with other experienced Dreamweaver's."

Sean dusted off his feet, stretching his arms back wildly, he leaned forward. "I feel great. Let's get moving. I'm ready to go onto the next test."

Chapter 6

"I can see why Samantha likes you," Elijah noted as he walked over to a wall nearby.

"What's this about?" Sean looked at the angel with peculiar eyes.

"I'll show you." So swift were Elijah's movements, his feet elevating him on the wall at an angle. Shifting his body weight, he jumped on the ground at the end of the curved wall.

"From one impossible task to another!" Sean's throat was dry as a desert. The exhaustion from the previous task was wearing down on his body. "What do you want me to do? You're talking about walking on walls sideways? How in the heck is this supposed to happen? I don't fully comprehend how to channel mana yet. I'm flying by the seat of my pants here."

"To be a Dreamweaver means you have to defy the reality you put in your mind." You think you can't do it because on Earth you saw the movies. Yes, we know what movies are. So you're sitting here looking at me, and you've already seen plenty of impossible things that you never knew could exist, so why not be able to walk on walls?" Elijah tilted his head sideways putting out two fingers walking on air. "Why can't you take the time to learn how to do this? If you want to see your beloved Tabatha, she needs to be a resource. And if Tabatha is your source, I think you can do anything because we finally found what makes you tick."

I remember her warm lips touching mine. Our trip to the private island with the three-star hotel near the ocean was divine. "I know she's my girl," Sean affirmed to Elijah, "and I'm going to keep that in mind."

"Good, now go ahead and try to run up the wall." Elijah pointed toward the white wall pulling back his finger like a bullet firing out of a gun.

"All right, here goes nothing." Sean started to run; his feet then quickly went sideways to run across the wall. He slammed into the ground, his shoulder hitting hard on the floor.

The whimsical angel pranced over to Sean his feet barely touching the ground. "Once again, reality is within your mind. Focus, be intentional with your thoughts. From what I hear, you drift off into random thoughts. You will die the second you get out there if you don't focus." Elijah pointed his index finger toward his head. "Nothing else matters. If you can do it, then you may have a chance of becoming a Dreamweaver. You may have the opportunity to be able to survive your first demon encounter."

Sean leaned on the wall panting. "I'm going all out for this. My mind hurts terribly. My body is throbbing with pain. I swear my head hurts more times than I can count. And it still hurts even though I'm not in my Earth body. I'm trying my best here, man. You keep busting my chops."

Elijah walked up and put his hand out to Sean. "I'm busting your chops so a demon won't be able to bust yours."

Sean looked at the hand extended out to them and took a deep breath. "Man," he said, grabbing the hand of the kind angel before him. "I understand what you're trying to do."

Sean sat there exhausted, leaning on the wall. "If this is what you have to do to become a Dreamweaver, then I don't want to see Anastasia." Sean sat there for a moment, realizing what he had said. He waited for the moment, thinking he would be magically transported to a place of torment. He didn't want to hear the screams again.

He closes his eyes for a moment thinking of Tabatha again and her hug and embrace. Sean's hands trembled... *I miss you, baby. I need you. I wish you were here.* The closest one who cared about him was Samantha, and he felt oddly close to Melody, who went out of her way to help him find a good place for lunch.

"Here, you must be thirsty." Elijah handed Sean a bottle of water with a big smiley face on it.

"What is this?" Sean asked Elijah smiling oddly.

"It's fizzy water, don't you know? It's the best water here. Take a sip. I am surprised no one's given it to you yet." Elijah opened his own bottle and took a sip, and smiled wide.

Sean looked at the big smiley face in black. He opened the bottle and took a sip. "This tastes like my favorite soda back home. But it looks like water." His fingers traced the smooth grooves on the outside of the bottle. "This place continues to boggle my mind. How in the world is this possible? This is the best thing! It looks like water, but it is a soda. I need answers!"

Elijah laughed almost spitting up his beverage. This is one of paradise's favorite drinks. It is called fizzy pop, and it comes from a fountain in heaven. It is supernatural, and it will always be your favorite drink. We get a limited amount here in the Dreamweaver Society. It is always gone every month. So we make sure to get all new Dreamweaver's at least one to know what the other side is like. There are so many other things in paradise I can't even tell you yet."

I know when I'm working for it, I can drink this every day, man, this will be amazing. "Weird, I don't feel like my stomach will be tied in knots because it's a perfect drink." Sean leaned his head back, gulping down the delicious pop.

"It is perfect because it comes from paradise," Elijah says.

"Do you ever get to visit home?" Sean asks the intelligent angel.

"Visit home? Oh, you mean like a vacation back to heaven. At times I get to go back, but our work keeps us busy, and we barely keep afloat." Elijah's thumb slowly graced his chin. "Demonic presences on Earth are getting larger, so the stronger angels are being sent there. Even those that train here, especially the Dreamweaver's, have been sent to fight and deliver strongholds. Cities are filled with wickedness." Pausing for a moment, there was a cracking noise, the angel shifting his neck to the right. "If those cities overflow with wickedness the worst could...."

"What do you mean what would happen?" Sean looks curious at the angel.

"I don't wanna overwhelm you. I do miss paradise and get to go every now and then." Elijah smiles then he finishes his beverage as well.

"Thanks for sharing. I appreciate it, Sean affirmed. Makes me feel human to have an actual conversation. Most of the conversations I've had here have been a mystery." Sean gave the bottle to Elijah. "Thanks for the drink. I'm gonna attempt this again," he bellowed.

Elijah put out his hand as his bottle levitated toward the trash can before being gently deposited.

All right, I can do this, I can do this. Sean ran forward, put his hand on the wall. He felt his body belay toward the wall. He stepped slowly. Smack! He hit the ground hard rolling over holding his left shoulder. *Damn!* "Almost there, almost there. I need to calculate to make this work." Sean thought back to his college dropout days. Walking up he observed the wall and its curvature.

Elijah looked curious at Sean. *What are you up to?*

Sean then extended his arm against the wall. My arm is about two feet long. He slapped his arm on the wall numerous times around the bend. *The curvature of the wall is about thirty feet.* Sean dashed toward the curving wall's front, his feet belaying his body toward the ground. *Tabatha, I adore you! That's ten, twenty, and then thirty.* Leaping off the wall, he jumped on the floor, gripping his chest.

"I see you're trying hard to keep your emotions under control. You may genuinely grasp your spiritual energy when Tabatha is your focus. She is the one to whom you dedicated a great deal of your energy back home. However, you are far more capable than you realize. I can see why Samantha chose you, but mastering this concept will take a long time. You'll have to study and quit being so sluggish. Yes, I read your file; you are a slacker. However, I'm amazed, and I am not easily impressed."

"You only needed to do ten, not thirty steps on the wall," Elijah chuckled. "I want you to push your limits."

"You've got to be kidding me," Sean bellowed as he rolled on the ground, clutching his shoulder. "All of that, and I only needed to do ten steps."

"Well, it's only going to go get harder from here on out. So, take heart, and know that you must push yourself, and it your courage here today demonstrates that you have the potential to succeed." Elijah gave another double clap, walked over to him, and raised his hands once more. "Are you prepared for the final exam?" Before we proceed to the final test, I'd like to discuss how mana affects your actions and abilities both here and when you return to Earth and hopefully help people in your world." Mana is fundamentally what the spiritual realm is made of." Elijah took his fist, opening it wide, and then closed it quickly. "If you think negative thoughts, then your mana will be restricted."

"It reminds mean that when we don't eat right and take care of our bodies, bacteria and other things grow in our bloodlines," Sean said with a smile.

"You're getting it, but it's so much more than that." "So this section is to test your ability to understand how the spiritual realm works and the consequences of your actions," Elijah said, raising his two hands above his head, interlocking them. "With positive thoughts, your spiritual flow will be more substantial because you will be in tune with your body. The spiritual flow is required for attacking, defending, and for traversing the spiritual realms. As you can see, Dreamweavers are capable of flight, and those skills are difficult to learn."

Sean looked at Elijah, slightly dumbfounded. "I had to stay positive all the time to operate and use spiritual powers, or even attempt to become a Dreamweaver."

Elijah circled Sean, their noses nearly touching. "Certain people are better at spiritual disciplines, did you know? Some people have it. Don't tell me you can't achieve it, and it means you may have to work harder. It takes more than positivity, but focus. My first assessment of you, I found you pathetic."

"Thank you," Sean murmured under his breath. "Go ahead and rub it in because everyone has always said I'm pathetic. But I did it, and I never imagined I'd be able to."

"Let me finish," Elijah demanded. "However, in the last few hours, I've noticed you have an innate ability to love deeply. If you focus and use positive emotions that may have caused you pain or happiness on Earth, I believe you will be able to grow as a Dreamweaver and make a difference in your personal life. Isn't it true that the ultimate goal is to reach paradise? Everyone wants to get there, and I believe you can."

Sean stood there, his eyes swollen with moisture. *I desperately want to return to Tabatha, but the only way to do so is to be-*

come a Dreamweaver. *Without Tabatha, eternal life would be meaningless.*

"Now, let me return to what I was saying. When it comes to mana flow, you must be careful to keep your focus and your body in sync. This means you can't lose control or use too much mana, or you'll be useless on the battlefield. Furthermore, imagine that the demon you're fighting is far too powerful. What if the person is too far gone for you to help? Do you abandon them to die? Do you fail to complete the mission? Do you make every effort to save this person?"

The barrage of questions made Sean dizzy. *The noble response would be to fight.* "If I'm outmatched, I'll flee. I live to fight another day. If I die, I am no good to anyone. If I die in the dream world, The Void is next to visit." *Torture is not on my bucket list of things to do.*

"You'll flee to save your own skin... interesting." Elijah's nose twitched to the left as if he detected a foul odor.

"Would you like to fill me in on something?" Is fleeing for my life a form of desertion?" Sean quickly tapped his left foot. It is impossible to help someone who has gone too far, and others require assistance as well. According to what I've heard, there aren't enough Dreamweaver's to go around."

"Outstanding responses!" Elijah clenched his fist. "I don't want to overload you with information. If you need to make a quick decision about handling a situation, that could mean the difference between life and death for you or a fellow Dreamweaver. Remember the danger you will be going into." Elijah stretched and winked at Sean, who remained seated on the ground.

"How long does a Dreamweaver have to wait for salvation? That is, assuming I don't perish on the way." He let go a slight chuckle.

Elijah hissed. "I can't tell you that, but I can say it is longer than five years. It all depends on what happens in your trial, and I'm sure yours is coming up soon."

"My trial. Samantha hasn't told me anything about this. You mean they're going to put me on trial for what I did on Earth? Do I get representation?" Sean's mind raced as he slowly freaked out, his eyes twitching.

"It won't be until tomorrow, so you have all night to think about it, and I think you'll be fine. Samantha will be there to defend you, and it isn't a matter of winning or losing; but why you would be a valuable member of our society. Samantha is probably planning your defense as we speak."

Sean thought back to Samantha. *She was acting strange, and maybe she was worried about defending me. Perhaps she thought he was weak or a waste of space. I'm so much more. I can do this... for Samantha.*

Chapter 7

"I appreciate you taking the time to train me," Sean expressed gratitude to the gracious angel. "You were the most rational of all the angels I encountered today. Macedon was insane, and Emery tried to persuade me of everything. All of the questions she had on the test made me feel like I'd be thrown into The Void."

"Those two are over a century old. I suppose we're all eccentric in some way." He giggled. "However, you're welcome to come here and keep practicing." Elijah smiled as he moved his hand to the spot where Sean had fallen. "All you have to do now is figure out what to do."

Sean thought back to the terrifying fall, a lightbulb triggered in his brain. "I think I know what you mean."

"You must understand who you are and what this place is all about. When it comes to living here, the most challenging part is adjusting. Maintain your concentration. Thinking about Tabatha will help you focus. As long as you keep her in your mind, your mana will grow stronger."

"I appreciate it," he said. Sean bowed a broad smile on his face. Sean turned around and returned to the corridor where he almost died. *He told me I needed to find a way up.* Sean looked up the dark stairwell with small lights flickering on each wall. *It appears to be a section for an elevator.* He sat there for a moment, expecting something magical to appear, but nothing did. *What should I do?*

"Climbing is the only way to get to the top." Sean was look-ing at the wall with a big grin on his face. *Yes, I believe I am capable of completing this task.* He stretched back, recalling Macedon's ad-vice about honing his body. *Let's get started!*

Sean went back out and ran full speed up to the wall of darkness, putting his foot against the wall and then stepping out and jumping across the walls. *I believe I see the door.* Sean could feel his legs weakening. He pushed off the wall, concentrating on Tabatha with each step; his feet felt like they were planted firmly yet as heavy as cement. His breath was heavy as his only hope was the flickering sign above him. *I'm almost done.* He pushed his right leg back to the left wall leaping toward the door handle. Sean opens the door returning to the shopping mall.

He slid back into the commercial alley, his breath shortened. He straightened up, calmed himself, and closed the door. "I'm done today. I need a drink a real one!" He brushed off his suit of the dirt from the walls.

Several people walked by Sean, and they giggled at him. Many of them knew what he had experienced.

"It's all right," a man's voice said, "it happens to all of us." The young man put his hand out to Sean and gave him a smile.

I guess I'm not the first, and I won't be the last, and I can't be too embarrassed. Sean let go of the man's hand, watching him disappear into the crowd.

Sean took a peek around and saw that it was nighttime out-side. He began walking around the mall, rubbing his shoulder to ease the pain. He noticed fewer people at this hour since it was evening.

I'm curious as to what Melody is doing. Before exiting, he took a step around the corner and stared at the silver and marble floor. *Is there a way for Samantha to come and pick me up?* He stood there for a moment hoping his thoughts would summon his steadfast angel, and to his dismay, no one came.

I suppose I'll walk home. Sean raised his eyes to the heavens. The pink and purple clouds painted the sky. Taking a step back he continued onward, his attention fixed on Tabatha. *I adore you, sweetheart.* He dashed forward and sprang into the air. He then stretched his arms after drawing them in. His feet collided with the ground. Looking back he surmised it was around a thirty-foot gap.

Several minutes later...

As he approached a directory, he examined the map and found the housing district. He lowered his eyes to the little speaker at the base of the statue. *I'm wondering whether this is some form of help button.* He pushed it, and the machine responded with a voice.

"How can I help you?" the cheerful voice responded.

"Yeah, I was wondering if there is anyone who can take me back home? I'm new here, and I'm unsure how to get back. I'm sorry for bothering you," Sean said.

"Someone will be there soon to pick you up. Please take a seat on the bench next to you," the voice said sharply, hanging up.

"Thank you," Sean murmured as he sat down. He leaned back in his chair and gazed up at the stars above him. *Life? What exactly is it?* He pinched himself to ensure that he could still feel pain. *This realm seems like a second Earth. Who would want to leave here? Is paradise all that it is cracked up to be?*

"Hello," a voice cheerfully said.

Sean sprang into the air, terrified at what appeared out of nowhere, and spoke to him. "Wow, you're a unicorn!"

"Yea, I am, and I am your taxi. First time taxi fares are on us, and you get our premium taxi." With a grin, the unicorn lowered its head toward Sean.

"I don't know what to say." Sean was exhausted from his day of training.

"I like you," the unicorn said. "Now hop on."

Sean nodded and hopped on top of the white-horned beast.

"Hang on," the creature said. As it took to the air, its wings flapping furiously, rocketing up at lightning speed.

Sean was holding on to the unicorn's mane for dear life as it corkscrewed into the air and dove into a dense forest of trees. It turned left, right, up, and then a complete 360 into the air, flying straight ahead over a sparkling sea.

Why couldn't they have provided me with a helmet? Where are the insects? Sean was not pleased with the way his eyeballs were being blown out of their sockets, and he was fearful that his face might blow off as well.

The unicorn came to a halt. "This is what we refer to as the Enchanted Sea. It is a place where people come to reflect. They plunge into the sea to receive divine purpose, while others seek refuge in the water."

"How do they manage to survive? How did they escape drowning?" Sean asked as the unicorn flew low to the ground, and Sean was able to look directly through the water.

"Those people have accepted their true spiritual self. They are one with the mana in their soul. They can master their breathing and hold their breath for extended periods by slowing their blood flow."

Sean glanced up and observed the high-rise condominiums hidden amid trees and other distinct structures for the first time.

"Well, you said that entry-level housing, here we are. We travel all across our society. Bear in mind that this VIP trip will cost around 500 gold coins in the future."

Sean patted the unicorn on the head. "Oh, I'm sorry," Sean said, jumping off.

"It's okay! Back on Earth, you guys have horses, and you pet them a lot when they do well, so it doesn't offend me. If you want to thank me for the ride the next time, I don't need a pat on the head." The unicorn took off into the sky.

Sean stepped up around the corner and to his door, still astounded by the reflection of the sparkling water at night. A little blanket was put on a chair outside the front door. There was a letter with a lousy drawing and a box beside it. He picked up the letter opening it.

"Sean, I'm sorry I didn't get to spend the afternoon with you. Sweets from the best bakery in town are here. I know you like strawberries because your grandma always used them in baking when you were little. There are three strawberry pies and two strawberry cakes in the box. I hope they'll still be warm when you get here. I got them around 8pm . Most people spend a long time with Elijah. Take some time off. At nine in the morning, I'll be there to guide you to your court hearing. Your Guardian Angel is there for you. Samantha."

Sean closes the card, smelling a sweet scent from the box and blanket. The quaint medievalist room was how he left it, and his bed was neatly made.

Taking off his suit, he stepped into the shower turned the water on medium-hot. *Tabatha, I love you, sweetie.* Leaning on the shower wall, he tried to recall what had happened before he came to this new realm. *It's all hazy! I don't remember a thing.*

Taking a bar of soap, he was greeted with a pine-scented shower. For the first time since arriving, he was able to take a long shower, which allowed him the opportunity to pause and reflect.

Some of it is coming back. The night I was going to propose, I took her to a restaurant. That hibachi place was amazing. I remember her long black hair and pink-painted fingernails. She smelled like fine wine on a Sunday afternoon. Her touch sent my body into a frenzy. Before asking the question, I went to the re-

stroom to calm myself. His thinking became hazy as he bathed his body with fresh pine soap.

After turning off the water, he grabbed a white robe that hung it in the restroom's rear corner. He stepped out and headed straight to his bed, where he lay down. "I don't believe I have the energy to put on my pajamas," he reasoned.

"Tabatha," he said, Sean felt the world around him go black.

Chapter 8

Knock knock knock knock knock knock.

"Is he still sleeping? I still can't believe it." Samantha opened the door to see Sean in his white robe stretched out on the bed. *When he's asleep, he's adorable.* She rested her right fist on her neck, leaning to the right.

Walking over, she leaned over and looked at him. "Wake up, Sean," she yelled at the top of her lungs.

"What?" Sean leaped up, punching Samantha in the face.

Samantha sat there smiling at him. "I've seen you fall asleep and not set your alarm clock several times. I figured you'd fall asleep, so I came over sooner. I don't feel terrible about you striking me in the face. I feel a little bad for waking you up, but here we are." She rubbed her right cheek where Sean's fist landed. *It didn't hurt!* "We have around thirty minutes until you have to appear in court. You won't be wearing the outfit you were wearing the other day, and this is what you'll be wearing."

Sean's eyes rubbed together. Tabatha remained in his thoughts. "Sorry I punched you. I think I should get up and do my hair." Sean stood up slowly and proceeded to the bathroom to fix his hair.

He jumped in the shower, put on a shower cap, and washed his whole body in three minutes. He quickly wiped himself off and placed his arms outside the corridor. "Would you mind tossing me what you want me to wear?"

"I pulled it out of the box for you," Samantha said. She approached Sean, turned her back on him, and gave him the clothes he'd be wearing for the next several hours. "I hope you like it. I chose it just for you, and it's from a previous event you attended."

Sean took a glance at his clothes. It was the same outfit he was wearing when he died. Blue pants, pink shirt, blue tie, and blue sports coat. "This is perhaps the most expensive outfit I've ever purchased back on Earth. I recall going to the department shop early in the morning since I'm a procrastinator, and an amiable lady assisted me in figuring out how to wow her."

Samantha sighed. "I know you miss her, and we're going to court. Make an effort to convey your emotions. They'll want to know what you're up to. I can't give you too many tips since you're the one on trial, not me, but I'm sure you'll do fine. Are you almost ready?"

There was another small box outside, waiting for Sean to open.

I need shoes and socks. I suppose I can put on the ones I wore the other day. Sean began to stroll closer to the bed, looking at his somewhat muddy shoes from the events of the day before, which were highly scented with musk. Sean nosed flared, walking out of the bedroom.

Samantha stood up, a broad smile gracing her face. She handed Sean a white box with a bow on it.

78

Sean took a package, and to his astonishment, it contained a pair of brown shoes and blue socks. The loafers were identical to the ones he had purchased the day of his proposal to Tabatha, and they had a certain radiance about them.

"I had the greatest shoemaker craft them and apply his special polish them for you. They were a touch pricey, but it was okay." Samantha smiled as she clasped her hands together and rested her head on them, staring at Sean, who was almost in tears.

"Thank you very much," Sean said as he slipped on his socks and shoes. "Now I'm ready to dazzle, or so I hope," he said with a chuckle. "Let's go."

Samantha nodded. She opened the door, both of them walked out into the morning sun.

Closing his eyes, Sean was ready for Samantha to grab him and shoot up into the air. To his surprise, she pulled him close and flew gracefully into the sky.

"You weren't expecting that, were you?" Samantha proclaimed giggling softly. "Usually, we're always in a rush, but we aren't going too far. We are heading to the business district just north of here.

"I wasn't." Sean said, "everything here takes off so quick."

She turned right, bypassing the Enchanted Sea toward a forest town.

"What's there, and why are those people gathering food?" Sean looked as puzzled as a dog. Most of the food may have come from paradise, but this was a Dreamweaver's Society. There is still so much he didn't understand about where he was.

"Like on Earth, there's almost every job here in a Dreamweaver Society. Our food has to come from somewhere, and it's a little bit different from how Earth grows its crops. Tending to the land is still a process of reaping a harvest," Samantha stated.

"Does it still take time to grow and cultivate? Are those people working on going to paradise as well?" Sean asked his Guardian Angel.

"They are," she said, "exactly like you." Samantha gained momentum and soared ahead across a snow-covered peak. In the distance, there were skyscrapers everywhere and individuals flying through the air, and little contraptions that others were utilizing. They all seemed to rush and attempt to get somewhere as soon as possible.

He had no way of knowing which of them were angels or Dreamweavers. Sean gazed up at the massive structure with the initials 'DS' on it, and he imagined the initials stood for a Dreamweaver Society.

Samantha began to descend, and the structure became more visible. They arrived in front of the enormous building with a 'DS' in gold letters on it.

"Remember, this is the pinnacle of our culture. Consider it similar to a president or someone in authority back home. There are affluent people here, both Dreamweavers and angels. Do your best to make an effort to treat them with dignity if spoken to." Sean walked in behind Samantha, keeping close to her and fixing his eyes on what lie ahead.

Some of the individuals they walked by were tall, smaller, but almost all were in clothes like Samantha's. Sean looked at his own outfit; it did look a little out of place.

"I'm not gonna say a word," he told Samantha. The colors on the wall were bright blue, some paint was white, and the others were painted with brilliant rainbows. Each step felt like a mile. With Samantha beside him, he felt assured that he was in the right place and there for a purpose.

"What is the meaning of this building?" Sean leaned in closer, almost touching her suit.

Samantha "Well, here at Dreamweaver's HQ. Most are Guardian Angels, and a few high-rank Dreamweaver officers are on the council. Also, Alexis has a place here."

Samantha took Sean's hand and wrapped it around her as she flew up slowly.

Sean heard the angel's heartbeat, and it sounded like a human's. He remembered Samantha mentioned Anastasia created angels different from humans. He felt her hand on his head stroke in a tender way as they continued to fly up now near the thirty-fifth floor. *She really does care about me. All of this is mysterious. She has to know about Tabatha and what happened to me. I do remember hearing angels have more than one human to look after. Maybe she didn't have time to see what happened.* The thoughts continued to travel through his mind as he felt Samantha go forward and land on the fortieth floor.

"Are you ready?" Samantha started to walk forward with a tense look on her face; she was prepared for battle. Her eyes were narrow, and her usual smile was gone.

Sean looked up at his Guardian Angel. *I wonder what she's thinking,* Following her, they went to the left, and a large wooden door with language unknown to Sean's eyes appeared before them.

"Are you prepared to take the next step?" Samantha's gaze fell to Sean's trembling hands. I'm confident that you'll succeed. The angel patted him on the back.

Sean followed Samantha, who opened the door in front of him.

Sean remarked on how much smaller the space seemed. He sat in front of a big pillar, which had a chair and three more chairs to its right. There was a little silver chair with a leather seat as the doors closed behind him.

"Take a seat if you will," Alexis said in a standard tone turning around from an oversized chair above him.

Sean walked up and sat in the seat.

Samantha then went to the left of him. She took a seat in one of the four chairs.

"We are here to make certain of the status of Sean Wilton, who is seeking to become a Dreamweaver. This trial will look at his current situation here and the training he underwent to see if he can proceed forward in our society. If those who observe him find him undesirable to pursue Dreamweaver status. If there are no jobs better suited for him, then he will be tossed into The Void."

"That's unfair. What, is there an overload of humans here?" Sean looked over at Samantha, who shook her head, and he lowered his tone and looked up at the tiny angel. "I'm worried I'm not getting a fair chance."

"You will have your chance to make your peace," Alexis stated this calmly. "But first, we need to hear from others who noticed your abilities and talents." "First, I summon Macedon the angel to the stand."

Macedon, the massive, dark-skinned man from yesterday, walked out and stood in front of Sean, who was sitting in the chair in the middle of the room.

"Good to see you again, kid. You're not dead, so that's good. I'm surprised they didn't give you a hard time, or maybe they did, and I didn't hear about it. Let's get this show on the road."

Alexis glared at Sean her chartreuse eyes that cut into his soul . "Are you ready?"

Sean nodded, taking a big gulp.

"Macedon, when you're ready, go ahead." Alexis nodded and extended her hand to the massive, ripped guy.

Macedon had a smirk on his face as he stared at Alexis and Sean. "What is a man? A man is one who can take action without a second glance. A man is one who can slam his foe down for the count. Did I see this potential in Sean?"

Sean eyes rolled around in his head eventually settling on the muscle-bound man with a slight smirk. *I hope he doesn't slam me into the ground.*

"I thought there was a glimmer of hope! However, I did see a sluggish dude. If he's willing to be molded, he can change. However, he is not completely devoid of optimism, but he is readily misled by fleeting feelings. I would give him a chance. He will either die trying or won't try at all." Macedon flexed his muscles at Sean. "Don't disappoint me, kid."

Alexis looked at Sean with a slight smile. *Interesting!*

I thought I was a goner for sure. Sean's palm rested on his chest as he observed the massive Black guy sitting next Samantha. His eyes didn't even notice the beautiful red drapes hanging from the ceiling.

"Next up, we will have Emery assess the mental strength of Sean." Alexis scanned the corridor to the right.

An exuberant Emery entered the room and twirled before placing her hand on the floor. She glared at Sean, then turned to Alexis and shook her head. "Ma'am, I'm ready to go."

Alexis gave a nod and put her hands out.

Emery turned in a circle and ran up to Sean, looking at him dead in the eye. "You are not a good person," she said. "Your mental stamina is nil. You failed the test horribly."

Sean wanted to speak out but stilled his tongue.

The female angel ran toward Alexis and jumped into the air, letting go a fierce uppercut into the wind rattling the curtains above. "What an embarrassment, your honor! The Dreamweaver's Corps do not need a man like this. In the face of adversity, he would lose his composure. We're both aware that the spiritual world is a dangerous place to play about in. To put him in a life-threatening position would be an error of judgment on my part."

Sean looked at the ground, his mind racing. *I did all I could to make sense of the test. I guess it wasn't enough. Damn it, I can't do any more than that.* Sean had the sensation that he was swallowing a frog.

Alexis nodded, tapping her quill on the oak stand.

Emery approached Sean, her gaze fixed on him. "It's clear that you lack the mental capacity to make a rational choice. You are thinking with your Earth mind instead of your spiritual mind. In doing so, you put yourself in danger, and if not, others will get killed as well. I will not have your blood on my hands nor any others." The angel nodded and rushed away from Sean, doing a backflip and landing in the seat next to Macedon's. Her pink puffy polka dot dress resting gently around her.

Macedon cast a glance at Emery. "You really think he's pathetic?"

"Well, he is probably the worst I've seen in a while. He does have sincere convictions in his heart. Maybe he can amount to something but not yet." She cut Macedon a glance and a slight smile. "How are you?"

"I am doing well. I need a vacation, though." Macedon flexed his chest muscles shifting to the left in his seat.

Her eyes were focused on Sean. "I get it," Emery murmured.

One for me and one against me. I hope they don't kill my soul. Sean looked over at the hallway, and he saw Elijah emerge in a white and brown suit.

"Hello, Sean," the angel remarked politely as he looked at him. Elijah then turned to Alexis and smiled modestly. In her presence, he bent slightly and tilted his whole body.

Alexis leaned forward to hear Elijah's response, eager to see what he had to say.

"Thank you, Alexis! When I look at Sean, I see a man who is looking for his purpose. A man who is attempting to make sense of his present situation and the world around him. He brought about a maelstrom of feelings he can't even comprehend in our world, this culture, which he never knew existed.

"Why should we judge him so harshly for something he does not understand? Yes, the stakes are high, and demons are pushing harder than usual to destroy humans. We must continue to fight and move forward. This is what I see in Sean's eyes. The pressure we put on Dreamweavers is beyond what most spiritual beings can bear. They are supposed to be the best of the best here. Is Sean the best? Maybe not, but does he have the ability to understand the concepts of the spiritual realm and push though his fears and insecurities? I do believe the answer is yes! Should he falter, it would but our own fault. I certainly observed while training him that he had an aura of stubbornness about him." Sean looked at Elijah, trying not to blush.

Wow, I never thought he would say those things about me. Sean was hopeful for the first time in the trial.

Elijah took a bow at Alexis and walked forward to the seat where the other three angels were seated.

Alexis eyes met Samantha's, who was sitting behind Sean and smiled.

"Now it's time for the final testimony of Sean. Who is looking to become a Dreamweaver and earn his salvation. This will give him the ability to go to paradise after he finishes a certain amount of time of work, which will be decided by me after today's events. Samantha, if you will, the floor is yours."

Samantha stood up. She walked by Sean. She put her hand on his shoulder and looked up at Alexis. "Alexis, you know me. I am one of your hardest workers here in the Dreamweaver's headquarters. I'm always attentive, punctual and make every effort to ensure my clients, well, my humans, are taken care of. Can you give him the utmost treatment and care for the Goddess Anastasia would give them as well? As Guardian Angels, we are only a manifestation of her love, and I extend that love to every person I encounter.

"You know, lately, I have felt slightly overworked. Some choices have made people think we are losing our way as a society. Almost everybody knows Sean is not the most charismatic, caring, or emotionally stable person. I see so much more than all of you see. I've watched him since he was a young child and now he is thirty-two years old. However, I feel that with the correct instruction and guidance, this young man may become an accomplished Dreamweaver." Samantha gave him a wide grin as she stares back at him.

Sean put his hand to his chest and bowed. "Yes. My purpose is to find Tabatha and hopefully relay a message to let her know I'm okay. Alexis, we were about to get married, and I died suddenly. I really have no recollection of what actually happened, and I'm hoping to find out information and earn my way into paradise. And this is one of the reasons I am trying so hard. As you can see, despite my lack of aptitude or talent, two of the three angels over there saw that I made an effort."

"You can see, Alexis, Sean is determined and cannot be underestimated. I believe in time, he will have the ability to harness his talent, skills, and abilities. And it's hard, but he will also seek the truth to what actually happened when he died. Samantha nodded her gazed fixed on Alexis.

Do you actually want to know what happened to you, Sean?" Alexis stared down at Sean from her podium and intertwined her fingers.

Sean hesitated in his speech. "Honestly, I just want to know if Tabatha's okay. I want to see she's happy and well maybe to see if anybody came to my funeral."

A tapping sound is heard from Alexis's fingertips. "Have you forgotten that dwelling on the past serves no purpose? No matter how deep the questions are in your heart, if you hold onto the past, you will not be able to unlock spiritual truth within you. You will not be able to use your mana and a way to not only save other humans but to protect yourself in the spiritual realm. This is a sign of immaturity."

"You know, humans are naturally curious creatures," Samantha said, pointing toward Sean. "All he wants to know is what happened to his love. He still has those deep emotions, and I saw from the records, he was able to walk on the walls with Elijah for twenty-five to thirty steps before falling. He has talent, and I believe we can use him to wage war against the demons, but it takes time."

Alexis said, looking at Sean, "I do understand what you are saying, Samantha, and I respect your opinion. Right now, it's three to one. Elijah, Samantha, and Macedon are in favor of Sean going forth with his training. Emery is the one who is opposed. I will take this all to deliberation. I will have an answer for you this afternoon. Is there anything else you would like to present, Samantha?"

"No, thank you for your time, Alexis. I'm thankful you gave me the ability to speak and let Sean know what is on my mind."

"There's something more I want to mention." As Alexis drew out a huge book and a gold pen, she cast a bemused gaze about the room. "Everyone in the room knows that changing a human's fate is a grave sin. Each record is reviewed by me, and I make the final decision on who deserves another shot."

There was a silent hush over the room as Samantha looked back at Sean with a slight smile and put her thumb up.

"Samantha!" Alexis said with a stern voice, "you are charged with plagiarism to alter an executive-level signature, thus changing the destiny of Sean."

As Sean saw his Guardian Angel, he sat there with his mouth gaping. *Why? She saved me for what reason?* As he began to feel dizzy and close to passing out, he began to ponder the possibilities.

Chapter 9

"He was supposed to go to The Void because he is not worthy of being here," Alexis said.

Sean stirred up, trying to hold in his anger. "You can't."

"Silence," Alexis said, her eyes ablaze not looking into Sean's direction. "This matter is above your understanding." Alexis adverts her eyes to Samantha with an intense look.

Samantha smiles at Sean as she glances back at him. "I have no remorse at all for giving you another opportunity," She remarked.

Two angels with white masks and blank expressions entered the room and placed golden chains on her wrists.

"Your actions have made me totally disgusted," Alexis bellowed. "As a Guardian Angel, you'll be stripped of your powers and bound."

Sean wished he could smack Alexis in the face. Samantha had to have rescued him for a purpose. *Why is she unable to speak? Why isn't Alexis allowing her to speak?* Sean's thoughts were racing.

To get closer to Samantha, he jumped over the table where he was sitting and ran toward her with open arms.

"You shall not touch," one of the angels said, putting out his hand.

Sean wanted to give his angel a hug, he shifted his feet dodging the hand of the large angel.

Elijah let go a slight smirk, impressed at Sean's antics.

After turning around, Samantha noticed Sean's firm grip on her arm. "Don't worry about me. I'm sure of what I did."

Sean felt his eyes start to trickle with water. Tears flooded his cheeks. He held onto the tall angel tight, rubbing his head into her arm. "You can't go. What am I to do? I don't know who to put my trust in.

"Trust in the ones who love you. I love you, and Tabatha adores you. Trust in us and use what you were taught here to find your way to her." Samantha's eyes moistened.

She's crying..I've never seen her cry. Sean felt his body being stripped from hers as he was thrown back across the way. He concentrated flipping in the air as he landed on the ground, feet up, looking at the two tall angels. "Is that all you got?"

Sean's pathetic effort to stand in their way was ignored by the angels. They led Samantha away from the corridor where the angels had appeared, holding her tightly in their arms.

Sean stood there staring at Alexis, knowing he had no right to challenge the lead angel in a Dreamweaver's Society.

It's not fair. It's not fair. He felt dizzy as he walked over to Elijah, Macedon, at Emery.

"Sean," Alexis spoke; looking at him she opened the book. "You are an anomaly, and therefore not supposed to be here. I will make an exception for you to pursue your status as a Dreamweaver. Make one mistake, and you will be tossed into The Void. You need to be on your best behavior while I investigate this matter. There could be more than meets the eye." Alexis looked at Sean and winks her right eye.

Sean raised his eyes to meet Alexis's, seeking to gauge her level of sympathy for his plight. *If there was an internal audit, Samantha had a wild wish to fall on the sword.* For the first time, Sean thought of the Goddess Anastasia and the power she may have. *If you are there, Goddess Anastasia, please comfort me, please help me see the truth in all of this. Is your judgment so harsh that you would take those we love away?*

Sean wept as he gazed at the angels on the left and screamed into his hands.

"Do not make a wreck of my courtroom," Alexis said. "You are dismissed, Sean, your journey as a Dreamweaver will start as soon as you step out the door. There will also be a package waiting for you at your house. All of you are dismissed."

The courtroom was quiet, and the two angels, Macedon and Emery, left the room from where they came.

Elijah slowly walked over to Sean and put his head on his shoulder. He knelt toward his ear. "Come on, man, you got to get going."

Sean lifted his knees off the ground. He stood up, looked Elijah right in the eye. "Can you do anything, Elijah? I don't know who to trust now; I don't know where to go."

"I saw who Alexis is. I don't think the other two did. I'll see what I can come up with on my end. But please know there is deception in the Dreamweaver world. You must be careful. Many with power do not want you to be here."

The duo walked out of the courtroom. They went into the elevator and went to the bottom floor.

Why would anybody want to hurt me? Sean looked at the unicorn above him, heading out the door. It was a taxi.

"You get used to it. This is home, but I would recommend well-needed rest. Would you like a ride home?" Elijah took his index finger and pointed it at him.

As his wings emerged from his back, Elijah clasped Sean's hand. Behind his outfit, he had a spectacular display of wings. They had a color that resembled that of the ocean.

Sean was amazed at the beauty he saw. He felt his body lift off the ground. The afternoon sun was shining over the industrial section of the Dreamweaver's Society.

As he struggled to fathom what had happened to his Guardian Angel, Sean gazed out at the awe-inspiring scenery. He glanced over to Elijah, who was smiling kindly and soaking in the views as well. "Thank you for taking the time to comfort me," Sean said.

"You're welcome! It's a pleasure as a fellow resident of the Dreamweaver Society and a Guardian Angel to serve humans. Humans are pretty much like little brothers and sisters to us. You're a bit different though, as you can see, we have the same type of body. Do you know anything about our origin?"

"Not yet! Hopefully, one day I can understand what this place is about. I can't operate if I have limited information. My dad always told me to grow up. With information it is possible to limit the risks we take in life."

"It seems you did retain some of the things your parents taught you. You've grown in a few days you've been here. I see why Samantha thinks so highly of you. As I said earlier, you do have talent, and if you continue to seek wisdom, who knows where you'll be in years. All right, are you ready for action?"

"Oh, I am." Sean had a big smile on his face as he looked at them. "Right, here we go."

Sean lost his grip and started to tumble toward the ground. "What the hell, Elijah?" Sean was indeed tumbling, the wind fluttering around him. He could barely think. *I can do this.* Sean tried his best not to look at the ground. *I'm going to die, there is no doubt about it. I'm going to hit a tree.*

Sean felt his body stop in midair as he opened his eyes to see Elijah beside him.

"I guess I pushed you too far. I was hoping the emotional trauma from seeing Samantha taken away would've given you the ability to fly or at least stabilize yourself in midair. I am still learning the extent of the human mind in our spiritual realm. Sorry I gave you a fright." Elijah stated.

Sean hands wave frantically in the air. "You did more than that! You almost made me pee on myself. That was really terrifying. You were right above me. Come on, man, you should have warned me."

"If I had warned you, then you would've held on tighter." Elijah chuckled, brushing his shoulder off.

Sean nodded. He felt the grip of Elijah's hand in his again.

"Can you take me home? Can we land there in the middle of the plaza?" Sean tightened his grip on Elijah, hoping to feel a sort of connection to the angel.

"Of course, man, I'll take you there." Elijah flew around the blue fountain with streaming water, landing softly on the ground. The angel let go of Sean's hand, he stood in front of him and put his hand on his shoulder. "If you believe all there is, is what you see, then you will never see all you are meant to see."

Sean stood there, his mouth open, nodding gently. "Thank you for taking me home."

Elijah put two fingers up as he turned around. "It's no problem. I will see you when I see you." Elijah lifted into the air at breakneck speed and disappeared from Sean's eyesight in a matter of moments.

He's charming. He didn't have to do anything, and yet he went out of his way for me. I think I can trust him. Can I trust him, Samantha? Can I trust him, Tabatha? You two are the only ones I can think of right now.

Sean sat on a bench. His lungs expanded and detracted inside his chest, looking up at the night sky, the stars too numerous to count. *I wonder what Samantha is doing now. I wonder what Tabatha is doing.*

He closed his eyes as he felt the cool breeze of the night caress his cheeks. *Tomorrow is my first mission. I wonder who they're letting me go with and what it is going to be like. They also said I would have a box on my front door.*

"Are you all right, man?" A cheerful-looking man with rosy cheeks and long blonde hair stared into Sean's eyes.

"Yeah, I think so," Sean murmured.

"I'm going to sit with you, bro. Looks like you could use some company," the man stated.

Before Sean could tell the man that he wanted to be left alone, he found himself in the company of the brazen individual.

"Look at the night sky. Isn't it majestic? Oh, by the way, my name is Percy."

"Nice to meet you, Percy," Sean said. *I have a busy day tomorrow.* Sean glanced over at the outfit with three gold stars connected to each other on the man's collar. The coat was white in color, so were his pants tucked into his long brown boots. *He's important.* He looked at the eyes of the kind man.

"Judging by the outfit, I can say you had your trial today; am I not, correct?" Percy leaned back putting his arms out around behind the bench.

"Yeah, everything went well, just as I expected." Sean shrugged his arms, trying to sound confident as if he had passed the initial trial to be a Dreamweaver.

"Let me guess anxiety, stress, and you have no idea what the hell is going on. Does that sound about right?" Percy said, laughing out loud.

Sean wanted to burst out laughing, but there was too much on his mind. Samantha went from his presence, and Tabatha was gone from his heart. "I'm still here. It's better than the alternative of being thrown into The Void. Tomorrow is my first mission, and I have no idea what to expect."

"Mission. Oh, so you're a Dreamweaver now. Quite the exciting job to be a Dreamweaver, isn't it? I hear all sorts of stories from those who come and go from the earth realms. They fight and kill those demons who would threaten the existence of the human population. Trying to make everybody depressed and kill themselves, those demons have nothing better to do than to go about their day tormenting humanity. Demons hijack human dreams. I shall call that form of torture dream possession?"

"Dream possession." Sean looked at the man with an intriguing look.

"It was probably in the initial book you got. It breaks down what a Dreamweaver does. What are they teaching everybody in training now?" Percy put his hands up and shook his head. "It's a little bit late to learn about the psychological aspects of the human brain. All I can say is if you apply yourself, you'll understand. I have to turn in myself, I've got a busy day tomorrow."

"Thank you for taking the time to talk with me," Sean said as he put his hand out to shake the man who sat beside him.

Percy smiled and put his fist out. "I'm more of a fist bump type of guy."

Sean changed his hand to a fist to meet Percy halfway.

Sean watched Percy walk away and disappear from his eyesight in a matter of seconds. He turned his eyes to the moon, stood up, and started to walk the quiet streets lined with houses. This was the first time he actually looked at all the houses in depth. Walking up to his home, he saw two items outside his door. On the exterior of his house, he had a huge teddy bear and a doll of sorts. Despite Sean's best efforts, the doll remained mute and did nothing. His eyes traced the long blonde hair and blue eyes of the doll. It wore a pink dress with black leggings. *Interesting.*

Lifting the teddy bear, Sean observed the package that Alexis mentioned earlier. *Hopefully it's not a box full of books with the rules I must follow.* He then walked into the room of his house.

Placing the package down, he walked over and made a cup of decaf coffee. Stripping off his clothes, he stood there. *It's not fair. Dammit, it's not fair. Why does all this have to happen to me? They took away the one person who had any love for me here. My Guardian Angel is locked up somewhere. I want to go find her. I want to save her.* "I want to free her," he yelled at the top of his lungs. Surrendering his face on the ground, he felt the cold cobblestone. *Dammit, dammit, Samantha. What did you do? Why did you have to leave me? I need you here. I need your help to guide me. Who do I trust?* He took his fist and slammed it into the floor.

I trust Tabatha. I trust Tabatha, and I use her to manifest my mana. His eyes were hurt from so much crying, he wiped them. He heard the kettle on the stove rattle a little bit. Sitting up sobbing, he took his arm and wiped his eyes. He sauntered over and poured a cup of coffee into his favorite mug. Sean sat on the oversized couch which was as soft and as comfy as he remembered.

He opened the box to reveal a small watch of sorts.

Sean picked up the watch, golden in color with blue highlights. He looked at the watch and flipped it around observing the craftsmanship. He looked at it and made sure he wouldn't mess it up. He found a small instruction manual. It said, "Do not open until you meet with the first person who will lead you to your expedition." *Expedition. I guess they don't want me to touch it.*

Sean picked up a small book titled "How not to die in the spiritual realm." The book was blue. It had black writing on it. *Well, they sure didn't spare any expense on this one.* The cover showed a man trying to escape, with a sword driven through him by a demon. It said, "Prepare or die." *I need to read this more when I'm awake.* Sitting the book to the side, gleaming item left inside of the box. Lifting it up he observed noticed the glittering nature of the item. *It looks fancy.* It was pure gold and had his name on it in cursive.

Sean sat the gold card on the table and looked out the window. *I guess I need to get ready for bed.* Sean felt his eyes water and getting heavier. He didn't know what to think. His new life was too confusing, and he had no idea what to do, how to get ready, and who to trust. Tomorrow was the beginning of an unknown journey. *How do I get back to Earth from here? I guess it will be revealed when I get to the pad at 8:00 o'clock in the morning.* Sean closed his eyes, and he remembered he had to set the alarm clock. *Or maybe I could do a wake-up call.* He looked over to a small clock it had different alarm settings, cute, mild, and hardcore. *I don't think hardcore will be the best in this situation.*

Sean laughed slightly as he remembered he was exhausted from the day before. *Maybe I should take a shower in the morning. I don't want to be funky.* Sean was already sleepy, but he dragged himself from the sofa and slipped into the shower with his boxers on.

I totally forgot to take them off. I can't believe it. I guess at this point, I might as well leave them on. Sean sat there, feeling the warm water pour over his body. He could not tell the difference between the tears and the water as he stared at the ground in the shower. The shower was extravagant. It had huge walls and marble floors. It had what looked like a silver faucet and gold handles.

He was amazed at how beautiful it was. He cleaned his whole body and washed his hair. He enjoyed the sensation of being soaked in the warm water. He was sore from all the training, both mental and physical, from the other day and from the trial today and the turmoil of losing Samantha.

He stood there for several minutes, pounding against the marble wall, his fists became red, he hit more as if trying to kill a demon; *I'll learn whatever technique it takes to figure out where they took Samantha and where my beloved Tabatha is.* Sean sat there. His eyes gazed into the marble, his anger fuming. *I'm tired of being left in the shadows. I want to know what's going on here. There has to be more than what I can see. I have been told to keep my eyes open and be aware of what is happening around me and not to trust anyone.* Sean sat there and started to think more about finding the hidden mysteries in the Dreamweaver Society. *I know this place is good. I know there's nothing wrong here, but there must be snakes. Maybe if I move up the chain, I can get access to certain materials.* His body began to wrinkle, and he turned off the water.

That's too much thinking for tonight. Sean smiled slightly. *Samantha would tell me to go to bed.* He looked at his clock, and it was midnight. *I guess I should try to wear my robe. I never liked these back on Earth. I thought they were always itchy, and they kept me from moving around and when I would have my intimacy with Tabatha. Maybe she enjoyed sexy time. Perhaps I should have taken more into consideration of her feelings. She wanted me to enjoy the process of making love to her, and I was an absolute idiot. Maybe I still am. Perhaps that is why I'm here.* Inside the closet, he saw a few more robes; there were purple-red and black robes. Anyway, I like these robes. Sean pulled out a purple one and slipped it on. It felt like it was made for his body to fit perfectly. He was too poor on Earth to afford anything else. He thought back to the tailored suit that cost him $500 at a low-budget boutique in the city he lived in.

Sean lay on the plush bed, moving slightly. *Is this a waterbed? No, don't tell me it's a waterbed. They really went out and got me a waterbed. It's different from the one I used to have. Maybe they were waiting for me to see if I would fall into The Void, or perhaps they were waiting to see what would happen to me if I didn't make it.* The things I enjoyed on Earth appear here. I guess all the more reason to work hard.

Sean rolled around from laughing until he fell asleep. He felt the waterbed gracefully go up and down like the waves of the ocean. *Man, I really could get used to this.* Sean closed his eyes. His last thoughts were of Tabatha and Samantha, the two people he loved most in the world.

Chapter 10

"Wake up, wake up, cutie," he heard from the alarm clock. "Wake up, you are a beauty, you're so sexy, I want to tickle your nose. Wake up, buzz buzz." *This thing is super cute; I love this.* Sean was trying to put away the memory of what happened yesterday and trying to focus on the way ahead. *I can do this. It's time for me to push forward. I can't sit and sulk; I have to get going.* It's what Samantha would say, and ironically what Tabatha would say to keep going and never look back. Sean pressed the cute alarm doll turning it off. He looked over at the clothes he had set aside for today. It was a blue suit this time with a white shirt and a blue tie. It had the initials SW on it for Sean Wilton underneath the right breast pocket.

Sean crawled out of bed and walked over to the restroom and did his hair up, then curved it to the left and to the right, and eventually went for more of a laid-back haircut like when he would have a date night with Tabatha. He then put cream on his face and let go a small smile. *The pain is still there, but I have to push forward. Anastasia does love me, then she will give me the strength to carry on. Right, I guess I need to believe that everything I see here is real; I think she must be real. And I'd rather not get on her wrong side.* Sean walked over and put on his white t-shirt and slacks, and started to boil a cup of tea.

Knock, knock knock!

I wonder who could that be. Sean opened the door, and he felt two arms wrap around him.

"I can't believe I'm with you." Melody jumped around Sean and twirled in a circle hugging him again. "We're going on a mission today!"

"Wait, what?" Sean said, looking at Melody. "First of all, good morning, and I didn't know that if you worked in a post office you could also go on a mission."

"I am a Dreamweaver," Melody exclaimed, "I've been here for a while, and I'm training with my Guardian Angel to hone my skills. So I can shorten my sentence."

"What?" Sean said. "How long are you here for, and thank you for the hug. I appreciate it." She was there in front of him with a bright green dress and black leggings. Her pigtails danced down to her hips.

"I had my hair up yesterday when you saw me, but this is how long it actually is. It can reach all the way down to my legs, but I like the pigtails, it took me an hour and a half to get ready this morning, and by the way, I left you a note. I got the news yesterday that I was going to team up with you. Did you not read the letter!?"

"Where did you leave the letter? I got a box, but I didn't get a letter," Sean said, walking over and putting on the blue tie.

"I left a letter underneath the cushion outside. I thought it would be cute if you went on a scavenger hunt," Melody said, walking out and grabbing the letter. "I got news from my Guardian Angel that I am bringing you with me this morning. On our first expedition, two more experienced Dreamweavers will accompany us. It makes me feel bad that you didn't open the letter. Regardless, I'll open it for you. "

"Don't worry, I'll read it when I get back," Sean said. "Would you like some tea? I could put the kettle on for you. By the way, how long is your sentence?"

"I'm okay without the tea. I had a cup of coffee this morning. Can you swear you won't laugh if I tell you something?" Melody put her two thumbs together, looking at the ground.

"I promise I won't. I can't. I don't even know how long my sentence is. They didn't even tell me yet. Maybe it comes later, I don't know." Sean made a heartfelt gesture with his hands, addressing Melody, who stood in front of him with genuine interest. "I swear I'm not going to laugh."

"30 years." She squeaked up.

"Thirty years," Sean said, "what did you do, kill somebody? It's not funny. It's a little intense. I mean, you must have done something pretty bad to get so many years of postal duty. And you said it's probably the lowest job of them all. But I don't judge you. I've made plenty of mistakes. I was a lazy good for nothing guy. So if you did anything evil, then I wasted time, so I would never judge you for anything. No, I would like to hear your story sometime. It has to be pretty funny, right?"

Melody took a deep sigh as she tried not to smile. "Thanks for not laughing. When the time is right, I will tell you why I became a Dreamweaver. I work so hard because I'm searching for that too.

And I can see in your eyes you are as well, so let's make a promise. We will both help each other get the answers we want. No matter what, no matter what it takes, we'll have each other's backs. What do you say?" Melody put her pinky out with a cheerful smile. Her freckles flared up.

I guess maybe the goddess did listen. This is a significant turn of events. Maybe Melody knows some things since she's been here for a while. "Sure, why not?" Sean put out his pinky gripping hers. "I know the tricks. You know how the kids were back in the day."

Melody winked at him as she let go of her pinky. "All right, get your essentials. I'm going to be outside."We don't want to be late," she said, glancing at her gold and silver-accented watch. From here, it's roughly ten minutes to get there.

"You know how to get there already," Sean said. "You know everything, don't you? Give me a moment to put my shoes and socks on. I'll be right out."

Melody grinned as she ran out the door, eagerly awaiting Sean's arrival.

I'm glad she came. I would be in a world of hurt. We may have to pay for a taxi, and they gave me a card. I don't know if I'm gonna need it or not. Sean grabbed the card, put it into the metal holder it came in, and slipped it into his coat pocket. He put the sports coat on, blue in color, and walked out the door out into the morning's sunshine.

"What is that?" Sean asked Melody.

"Oh, this is my new and improved broom. It's called the Super Axle 5000. It took six months of saving up to afford it." Melody put up her right thumb winking her left eye.

She sure spends her money on exciting things. She must have nothing in her house, or maybe she's a minimalist, or she grew up poor. Sean thought about all the scenarios that came to his mind, and he found himself staring off into the sun.

"Are you going to get on, or you're just going to stand there? Come on, we gotta go." Melody hopped on the broom, floating in midair as she motioned for Sean to get on the back. "Think of it like a motorcycle; hold on to my waist, and you won't fall off. There are also two little pegs to flip like a bicycle and put your feet on and strap in."

Well, this can't get any weirder than it already is. Sean walked over. He put his hands around Melody's waist, which was exceptionally soft. *She smells like honeysuckles. She smells almost as good as Tabatha.* His cheeks flushed feeling the broom lift off the ground.

"Be gentle," Sean yelled as he felt the broom go straight up into the air into a corkscrew.

"I told you to hang on. When it comes to this broom, I'm still getting the hang of it." Melody went to the left and then to the right, and then into a complete 360. At lightning speed, they swung to the right over a group of residences and then proceeded straight.

"Are there any speed limits up here? What if you slam into somebody," Sean yelled. Sean held tighter, enjoying the sweet smell of Melody. They flew over the Crystal Sea and passed by a small apple farm where people were harvesting for the next season.

She flew slowly upward, passing above a structure. The structure was round in form, with the letters DS emblazoned on the top and a silver circle surrounding it. Sean had never paid attention to it before. It seemed to be far bigger than he had anticipated.

"What is that?" Sean said to Melody, who was preparing to land. There were numerous additional brooms and contraptions on the deck, as well as other persons who had landed on it.

"This is what they call "The Hub". Seriously, did you not read the book? This is what connects us to the realm. You go here to the send-off, and this is where we meet the two upper ranks to go for Earth for our first mission." Melody floated the broom up as she landed on the deck, latching it into place as she hopped off the broom.

"Take a look around at all the contraptions," Sean said, taking Melody's hand in his as he stepped up and leveled himself, his gaze returning to cold steel on the landing deck. "I don't want to fall down."

"Keep your eyes on me, and let's walk forward," Melody said as she took a skip and hopped into the silver-plated double doors.

Brooms seem like deathtraps. Sean glared at technologically advanced computers and screens. There was a radar and different knobs with signals going up. He walked along the long corridor, which had white walls and silver marble flooring.

"Do you know where we're going?" Sean asked.

"Yeah, it's right up here. We're going to dock #5, which funnels into the larger dock into the earth. All those rooms you saw back there track the barometric pressure between the two realms and find the best place for us to enter. The demons are also trying to block our presence on Earth. We have to make sure we get it right, or a monster might appear upon our entry into the world."

"How do you know all this?" Sean asked, and he followed Melody in.

"Good to see you again," a man said. "It seems like yesterday we were talking." The man chuckled.

"Percy," Sean perked up, seeing the one who spent time with him the other night, giving him wisdom. Sean walked up and shook his hand, and smiled. "It's good to see you again, too. I didn't know if I would ever see you again."

"Nice to see you again as well. I'm going to introduce you to my friend over here. Her name is Faye."

"Nice to meet you. I don't take too kindly to babysitting grown men. Step up or get left behind. I'm gonna tell you this once, so you better listen." Faye had semi dark skin, long black hair, and forest green eyes that intimidated Sean. She wore a dark black tank top, a brown bomber jacket, and gray pants. She had long brown boots on and a black cloak.

"Pay her no mind." Percy said, "she's mad because she didn't get to go on a vacation, and she has to come on this excursion, especially since the mission is a simple one. This should be an easy mission, but demons are cunning, and it's just the four of us. You two are novices, and you shouldn't be fighting a whole lot. We will take the lead. You just stay back and watch. At some point, you may be going by yourself; we're going to go deep into a novice dream. It shouldn't be too hard, but I want to be crystal clear if anything happens; you get to the nearest exit, take the door out, and get the hell out of there."

Percy was frowning as Sean gazed at him. Percy's demeanor was a shock. Before this, he had only met him once; while his demeanor was upbeat and relaxed, his face screamed caution and alertness in the spiritual world. Sean nodded as he took it all in.

"Now, we should really get going," Percy said with a big smile.

"Take my hand Sean," Percy said, putting his hand out. "What we're about to do is called a magical bond. You will be connected to me through until I let go of your hand. You will not get hurt; it may feel like you're out of control. All you must of hang on tight. This is gonna be a little crazy, but it will be a lot of fun once you get used to it. Are you ready!"

"Biometric pressure is ready," a voice said over the intercom. "Everyone, prepare yourself and have a safe journey, and we look forward to seeing you back."

Before Sean could say thank you, the floor opened below him, and his face felt the intensity of a speed he could not comprehend. "Oh my goodness," Sean yelled as he held on tight onto Percy's hand. He realized that he was within a tube of light. He was surrounded by a kaleidoscope of light that he couldn't keep up with.

"Can you hear me?" Sean listened to a voice going through his head. "Yeah, I can hear you, but can you hear me?"

"Yes, this is my spiritual art. I'm able to stream my thoughts into your consciousness by connecting hands. Are you okay? I know we're going quite fast, and in this tube, I wanna tell you that you're safe. Keep your eyes forward and experience it. This is what we call a vortex. This is the connection between the earth and the heaven realms. The vortex it's not too long, and we should enter through the earth's atmosphere here in a minute or two, but what do you think?" Percy chuckled, his laugh filling Sean's subconscious.

"It's gorgeous," Sean said, "and you can really understand what I'm thinking; this is amazing. Can I learn how to do it?"

"No, sadly, you cannot. This is my particular spiritual art," Percy said, "each human has a spiritual skill you are born with, and over time, you will understand what your spiritual art is. I use mine to warn people. I'm more of a background guy, but I enjoy helping people. I like to fight too, but my job here is to let help people. There is also a good training ground back home to hone your art. You're almost there yourself."

"I'm grateful for your help." As they approached a tiny village, Sean noticed that the colors had faded. There were lights like in a carnival, and they looked like they were 200 or 300 feet above the ground.

"Everybody, hang on. We're almost there." Elijah then put his arms out like he was flying. Faye flew over to him with Melody. They all connected hands and descended slowly before they landed on a rooftop.

"How fantastic," Melody exclaimed. "Faye, you are amazing! You two make a great team."

"I am pretty dang good," Faye said. "Percy and I do make a good team, and we work together often. I was about to go to the hot springs and work on my skin a little bit. Even though we're in the afterlife, I still want to make sure my skin looks good," the up-tight Dreamweaver stated.

"All right, everybody, look alive. We can enter through here," Percy said. Percy walked through the window, and Faye and Melody followed.

I feel like they're all part of an inside joke I don't know about. I can stand on top of this house and not fall through, but they just went through the window. He clapped his hands on his face three times. *I should have paid more attention in physics class. Why am I not falling through it?* Sean stood there looking at the glass window covered in condensation.

"Are you coming?" Melody said as she put her head through the glass.

I'm stumped," Sean said. "Why did you go through the glass? I mean, how did you do it?"

"You just do it; you're a spirit being now. You can walk through the glass, and you can go through the top of this building.

But you have to focus." Melody put her head back through the glass disappearing from Sean's eyesight.

I feel like she's been training for this way longer than I have. Ok, here we go. Hopefully I will not get glass marks. Sean walked up. He put his hand through the glass, then his whole body. He entered the room. He saw a child in bed and a mother beside him.

Percy looked back at Sean, Melody, and Faye. "Demonic pressure is at a 2.9," he said to the three of them. "We have about four hours until daylight. The quicker, the better." His eyes traced the group behind him with concern. "You have a limited amount of time before the dream world collapses, so we must get in, exorcise the demon, and get out of there. This should be an easy one since it's 2.9, but things can quickly change in the spiritual realm. We always have to be on our guard. All right, everybody, hang on to my hand."

Sean wanted to ask many more questions. However, as Sean grabbed Percy's hand, he felt himself ready to pass out. There was an instantaneous darkness that enveloped his soul.

Sean opened his eyes and felt like he was going to throw up. He didn't know if everyone experienced the same nausea. He saw nothing but bright colors around him, and they were in a sort of tunnel of sorts.

When Percy unlocked his watch, he glanced back at Melody and Sean, then nodded his head. "When you go into the spiritual world, it's important to prepare your heart for it. You're both definitely dizzy and on the verge of passing out, but try to concentrate on your breathing."

"I am okay, how about you? I may be a little bit stubborn today, but I'm not gonna let you get hurt in any way." Percy walked over to Melody and Sean, who were huffing a little bit.

"I do feel a bit unsteady," Melody said as she tried to walk to Sean. "Hold me a little bit, won't you?"

"I can barely hold myself," Sean stated.

"Breathe deeply. The transition from the spiritual world to the demonic domain is jarring. When you get acclimated to the pressure, you'll be okay." Faye grabbed both novice travelers by the shoulders and held them there.

So this is the presence of a demon. Sean put his hand on his head, steadied himself, and he held on to Melody's hand rather tight. "Are you okay?" he looked over at her.

"Yeah, I'm all right," Melody said. She lifted her self off her knees.

Sean stood up straight, sweat pouring from his head. "Okay, I got this. I think I'm ready."

Percy looked back at the three Dreamweaver's. "Our mission today is a twelve-year-old child, and he doesn't seem to have any medical anomalies. It would appear he was under a lot of stress trying to live up to his family's potential."

"Stress can do a lot of harm to the body," Faye said. "This isn't the first time we've seen young children suffering because of their parents' expectations of them. It's quite sad. Actually, I hate seeing children in pain, and this makes me stressed. She let go of Melody's hand and smiled. "You ready?"

"Yeah, I'm ready," Melody said.

Sean smiled as he walked up next to Percy. "So, what's the plan? What do we do now?"

"As you can see, this is the world which the child's mind perceives. It looks like we're in a long hallway filled with giant blocks. I think maybe this is his innocence trying to combat the stress," Percy stated.

Sean looked over, and he saw the letters A&B on the blocks. Sean looked up and saw letters on top of them. *It doesn't seem too bad.* He ran forward as he felt his body slam into the adjacent wall. Sean turned around and was shocked to see a crimson glove retracting in preparation for a second strike.

"Get down now!" Percy yelled.

"Sean!" Melody started to run toward him.

Faye grabbed her from running forward. "Stay put, okay?"

"But!" Melody stood there clenching her fist, gazing into Faye's eyes.

Sean narrowly ducked as the glove barreled forward toward his forehead.

Percy ran forward, manifesting a bronze sword out in the air and sliced into the hard metal, stopping the fist from striking at Sean again.

"Thank you," Sean said, looking up at him trembling.

"Don't mention it," Percy proclaimed, "but please be warned, even though this is a simple mission, don't go running forward. That was really dumb! I don't want you to die. We don't know what type of magical enchantment that was. Faye, check him out."

As Faye moved closer to Sean, she bowed her head to gaze into his eyes. "I don't see any distortion of magical power or any signs of possession."

"Good," Percy said, "Please let me lead you to the next point." Percy walked forward. He looked carefully at each block, and he quickly observed where the spring came from. "There is powerful spiritual energy here. I can see why this young man is struggling. He has his defenses up. This block has the letter 'K' for knockout. His defenses are a little bit out of control," he said.

How embarrassing to almost get knocked out by the letter K and it was a boxer's glove. Sean nodded his head in agreement, trying not to show his embarrassment. Melody came up to him and wrapped her arms over his shoulders as he was clutching his head. "Are you okay?"

"Yeah yeah, I'm good. I am little shook up." Sean shook his head.

Faye raised him after taking one glimpse at him. "Wow, that was a stupid idea! Please, please, please don't do it again!"

Sean nodded, his gaze lingering on Faye as he tried to keep his grin in check.

"Percy, you said there are times when our personal situations can cause an influx in the spiritual realm," Melody said, walking up behind him, looking into the square hole from which the punch spring came from.

"That is correct," he said, feeling the outside square again and looking inside. "You need to be wary even if it's a weaker demon; you wanna always be on your toes. Many Dreamweaver's die because they can't know for certain what is actually before them." Percy looked back at Sean, casting him a slight stern glance. "Make sure you check every nook and cranny before you walk forward," Percy stated. "Running into a situation, especially where there's a demon who could lead you to your death, and then you get cast into The Void. Remember, none of us are saved by the grace of the goddess yet, so we really have to be careful."

Leaving the square, Percy walked forward as the three Dreamweaver's followed behind him.

"That's why we tread carefully. Apparently, this young man doesn't want to be found," Faye said.

Percy walked forward, pressing his foot gently on the tile in front of him. The letter 'S' slipped open, and it revealed a floor full of spikes of different colors.

"That is unsettling," Sean said as he investigated the hole. "It's so cute and colorful, but it's also full of death. Talk about a kid with a rich imagination. I would hate to be impaled by spikes."

"Demons like to play all sorts of tricks, so make sure you are always on your guard," Faye said, punching him lightly in the shoulder.

Sean nodded, rubbing his shoulder.

"Don't worry, I got you," Melody said, pulling out a small bandage and putting it on Sean's shoulder.

"Thank you," Sean said. *It didn't hurt much. It was a kind gesture, though.*

"You two watch closely," Percy said, manifesting his sword again. Percy ran forward, jumped over the spike hole, and ran across the wall.

Faye followed up, running on the tiles below them.

In a moment's instance, several red punch gloves with springs were all over the place. Percy weaved in and out, cutting each metal contraption off with a brute elegance.

Oh my goodness, that's amazing. He was following all of Percy's movements. Percy was jumping from wall to wall, slicing each one with the slightest bit of effort. He noticed Faye running across the ground and putting a sort of texture or protective layer over the potholes where the spikes were.

"You two come along," Percy yelled. "Follow behind us quickly."

Sean looked over at Melody and nodded. "Let's go," he said. The two less experienced Dreamweaver's followed them. They bounced off the small sticky material covering the hole.

"It's like glue but not like a spider's web," Melody said as she bounced up and down on it.

Faye looked back, annoyed at Melody. "You need to stop playing around. It's there for a limited time. If you don't want to die, keep moving."

Sean and Melody ran forward as quickly as they could. The walkway curved and then upward as they saw the wreckage of springs and different materials from the walls that would have led to their certain death.

Sean's eyes widened as he noticed Percy duck underneath and slide underneath a glove. Sean liked what he saw. He admired Percy's movements and wished he could have manifested a sword for himself, but they weren't to have any weapons, according to what Melody told him in the letter.

"Good, you two come here. There shouldn't be any more traps," Faye said with a smile. We took care of them all.

"Great," Percy said, wiping his hands together. "This time, it's good to get a break from the more complex cases. I can really let loose to be more relaxed."

Melody and Sean looked at each other and shrugged their shoulders, thinking the same thing. They were terrified of falling into pits, and trying to run on the walls and keeping up with them was almost a meaningless task.

Percy walked up, and he opened the door revealing a large open area. It looked like a meadow of sorts, but it had different toys in it. Rocking horses and clapping monkeys were among the grass. Everything seemed to be illuminated by a faint light in the distance. A strange language was spoken by the warped toys, and their faces swung about slowly as if in anguish.

Sean looked at the possessed toys, and then he looked back at Percy and Faye for an answer.

This is what happens when a demon takes hold of one's consciousness. Sean tried to focus as he observed the demented toys.

"If possible, we try not to destroy anything in the dream world. We're here to kill a demon, but there are times where collateral damage happens," Percy stated.

The meadow was bright with flowers, and it looked like the flowers were crying.

Melody bent down and looked at the flower. "What's wrong?"

"My mom said I can't play unless I master a math problem, and I'm scared. I'm nervous," the flower said.

Sean looks at the flower, its seedy mouth moved back and forth. "Don't worry, kid, we're gonna make it all right," he affirmed.

Percy looked back at the two who talked to the flower. "Wait, you two can help."

I'm delighted you can help me, but it would be better for me if you died instead!" The flower expanded tenfold in size, its face expanded, and a slimy tongue emerged from between its teeth. Melody was snatched by the flower and flung into the air.

"Help me!" Melody screamed.

What do I do! I don't have a weapon, so I will go bare-knuckle. "You bastard, let her go!" He ran forward and punched the flower right into its chest. The flower bounced back its tongue, letting go of Melody in midair.

"I've got her," Faye said, leaping into the air and landing a few feet in front of the oversized weed.

"Thank you," Melody wept.

"No problem," Faye said as she put her on the ground.

"You two stand back," Percy yelled. Running forward, he swung his blade severing the legs of the flower.

The flower then magically shrunk, laying on its back in the grass.

"Where did it go?" Sean looked around, but the giant flower was nowhere to be found.

"Behind you," Faye yelled.

Sean turned around to see the massive flower grow back in front of him, its teeth bared toward him. "Oh my god," Sean yelled. Sean slid underneath the flower, narrowly escaping the razor-sharp leaves barreling toward him.

Percy ran forward and put his sword in between the teeth of the flower, turned it sideways and slit its mouth open. The flower let out a wild screech as it wobbled back and forth.

"Faye, do it."

"You got it," Faye said with a smile.

Faye looked at Melody with reassurance, and then she ran forward, leaping into the air.

"We're going to get it before it shrinks back down," Percy yelled.

"You got it," Faye nodded as she did a front flip and barreled the heel of her right foot into the head of the flower.

Percy ran up underneath the beast and slid his sword, cutting up toward the mouth of the flower. The flower screamed and disappeared into ashes.

Chapter 11

Sean turned around in time to see the spectacular double-team move. *So this is a demon, or at least it looks like it's demon-possessed.* He looked in awe at both Faye and Percy. "You guys are amazing, and I mean it. So, can you tell Melody and me how that creature could reform and regrow?"

"We have to keep going," Percy said, "but I'll explain along the way. Also, I'm pretty impressed you could attack a demon with your bare spiritual fists. It says a lot about you, man. I'm pretty impressed."

"I think so too," Faye said. "I don't give compliments often. It did have some tricks up its sleeve. For example, like Percy was saying, the rules of the demon in charge meant the flower could use the demonic energy to grow back indefinitely unless we killed it."

"Though certain demons have different characteristics, they take up their power from what we can understand to do harm. With Faye and me, when I manifest my sword, it takes mana. We have to be particular in how we attack," Percy explained. "Usually, going in pairs is better than going alone. But these days, we are short on Dreamweaver's, and a group like this will be rare to see if it is not in a training scenario."

Sean wiped his forehead. "I am thankful we had a group this large. I have no idea what I would've done. Its teeth almost had me. What would have happened if it clamped on me?"

"Oh, your soul would turn into nothing, and you would eventually go straight to The Void," Faye said, "but we can't let that happen to our precious little trainees, right?" She chuckled slightly, looked at him, and made a snarl sound with her mouth.

She's scary! He was glad she was there. She had tremendous physical fitness, and he noticed her calves were huge, and she was able to slam her leg with no problem in midair and twirl like a gymnast. Even though she was a bit cocky, Sean was impressed with her abilities and how she appeared to care about him despite the insults.

"Thank you for saving me," Melody said as they continued walking, "its tongue was all sticky and slimy. It was gross. I'm gonna have to change my outfit when I get back."

Walking forward through the meadow, they came to an intersection with a large tree, and the tree was also weeping. "Everybody, be on your guard," Percy said, walking forward with his sword in his right hand. "Oh, wise tree, can you point us in the direction of the demon haunting this boy?"

The tree sobbed, and it could do nothing but look at the ground and mumble in an unknown language.

"I guess this is not going to get us anywhere. We have to keep moving," Percy said. "That tree is nothing but a forgotten soul here, and his spiritual energy tells us the boy is lost, even more, we need to save the child and quickly."

"Do we know how long he's been sick?" Sean asked Percy.

"There is really no way to know," Faye said. "The spiritual distortions are worse when the human is having a hard time dealing with their own insecurities."

"This is serious stuff. The trees and the flowers are all part of a more enormous scope of the human subconscious," Sean stated.

"You okay back there, Sean?" Percy looked back and gave him a smile.

Sean nodded slowly, his eyes glaring at the ground. "I am almost used to the demonic pressure. You said this is a lower demonic pressure, right?"

"Yes! This pressure was more of a shock to the system, and it could really overwhelm you. There have been those who could not even move when they were put into a situation like this."

"I can see why," Melody said with a slight smile. "I am getting used to it. It's not too bad, but I don't know if I can take any more pressure."

"Don't worry; you will get used to it over time." Faye walked forward and looked at the large building. The pressure was building there. It appeared to have a purple hue emanating around it.

Sean looked at the two-story gingerbread house with a chimney of candy canes. *What is up with that house.*

"I will go in first," Percy said. "If they are going to ambush us, it will happen there. Everyone, get behind me." Percy went up to the handle at the door. He put his ear to the door and didn't hear

126

anything. Looking down at his watch, the demonic pressure was already at 5.5.

Percy heard a sound from the house. "Everybody, get back," he yelled.

"How dare you come to this kingdom and try to rid us of what we have come to call home?" a voice hissed.

"What the hell?" Sean said, running back. "Is there someone in the house? What in the world is going on?"

"We need to find a way to get inside because if you're fighting a house on the outside, it will be meaningless. You two, get back. Faye and I will handle this." Percy ran forward, trying to grab the doorknob.

"We can't sit here and do nothing," Melody said, looking at him. "They're fighting a freaking house."

"I know," Sean said, "but we have no weapons."

"Hold on, I may try to do this. Give me a second." Melody closed her eyes. She put her hands together, chanting a prayer.

Sean looked at her and noticed something starting to form in between her hands. *What is she doing?*

Melody chanted for a few seconds more then something popped into her hands.

"A revolver," Sean said as he looked at Melody holding a pistol with six bullets. It didn't look like regular bullets to Sean. They were red in color with a dragon print on each one.

"How did you learn to do that?" Sean asked her.

"My Guardian Angel has been teaching me how to harness my mana. It's hard work, especially after a long day at the post office. I've been working and trying hard to create a revolver." She took the pistol, put in the six bullets. "I will try to shoot the door, so you can get in."

Sean felt worthless as he looked at Percy and Faye attacking the house. He looked over at Melody. *I really have nothing to offer. I can't go punch the house. What can I do? What can I offer?*

"Get out the way, everyone," Melody yelled, "I'm going to blow the door open."

Faye looked back and ran, dodging to the right of the enormous fist that was slamming into the ground next to her.

Here goes nothing! She pointed her revolver at the front door and pulled the trigger. Boom boom. Two shots rang as the house leaped to the left. A bullet hit the door and caused a massive explosion sending wood across the meadow.

That was smart; it's like a scene from a movie. This is crazy. This is happening in the real world. I wonder if I was ever possessed. Sean's feet wanted to move, but he had nothing to offer.

Two more shots rained out from Melody's revolver. Boom boom! They hit the front window shattering it into a million pieces.

Percy looked back, his face grimacing in pain.

The house swayed back and forth, and then it eventually tumbled toward the ground.

Sean started to run forward without even realizing what he was doing. *I have to do something; I have to contribute.* Sean ran to the front of the door, unaware of the danger he put himself in.

"Don't do that, you stupid idiot," Faye yelled, running toward the door.

"Good work," Percy yelled, looking back at Melody, giving her a thumbs-up.

Who am I looking for? The walls were gray in color, and there were distortions everywhere. The paintings on the wall spoke to him, saying hateful things about who he was and why he was there and that he should kill himself and no one in the spiritual realm was worth saving. *Samantha, be with me.*

Sean walked to the back of the house, running up a flight of stairs moving at a fast pace. He leaped up the wall, gripping his hands into the wood. *Ouch.* Pulling himself up the wooden wall, he saw a door before him with a purple hue surrounding it. *That has to be it.* Taking his hands, he brushed off his suit and straightened his tie. Turning the door knob slowly, his eyes fell on the dark shadow of an overweight man. "So, you're a demon," Sean said, putting his knuckles together.

"Foolish Dreamweaver, you are nothing but a swine. You can't defeat me," the obese man said.

Sean was scared. There was a black shadow coming out of the stubby demon staring at him, its eyes yellow and its tongue red.

Sean shifted his gaze to the left, where he saw a small child, no more than five years old, lying on the floor. His whole body was trembling and convulsing.

Sean clenched his fist as he ran forward, slamming it into the man's face. All he could do was continue to hit the demon's face over and over. "You have no right to do this to a young child!"

Sean felt his body slam back into the door. The demon hissed and jumped out of the window nearby.

Damn it! Sean pushed his hands into the ground, lifting himself up. He darted toward the window then saw the demon fall to the ground.

Percy was standing above the demon, his sword covered in blood. The demon disintegrated into thin air. The house slowly started to disappear.

This is going to hurt! Sean looked down at the ground, which was becoming visible through the wooden floor. *What is this!* Sean felt a pleasant sensation spread across his whole body. The home vanished in an instant, leaving him encircled by a bright light.

Percy winked at Sean as both of them slowly floated to the ground as the bright light disappeared around the two male Dreamweavers.

"Thank you for freeing me," the child said. "I can now live free without fear of my parents judging me. I've been so worried about myself, but I couldn't wake up. I forced myself into a coma with fear. Before I knew it, the demon had taken over my heart and my mind, and I could not do anything about it. Thank you for saving me."

As the youngster launched into the air, a dazzling light engulfed the whole area surrounding them. A child's utopia, with toys filling the space with delight laid before them.

Melody looked up at the clouds; her cheeks flared red. *This is the ideal image of a relaxing night's sleep. I'm so happy this child has found some sort of peace. I lived in such fear. And now, to see the demon or demons threaten this child's existence brings everything full circle. Hopefully, I can find peace as well.*

"This is what dreams look like," Percy said. "Without a demon's influence, a human is supposed to dream good dreams. But so many humans live in a pit of depression, and it's our job to bring them out of it. Take note of this, Sean and Melody. This is your path to salvation and heals the heart, but it offers you a better understanding of what it means to reflect on your human existence from a higher viewpoint."

Sean nodded; standing in awe at the beauty around him, he noticed the tree that was weeping a while ago. It was adorned with an abundance of bright red apples. However, he was aware that they would require time to mature before he could harvest them. They have been in the dreamscape for some time, and as much as he wanted to go, he didn't want to get lectured by Percy or kicked by Faye and her amazing acrobatic legs.

"Whats our next move," Sean said.

Faye looked over at Sean with a slight smile. "Now, we plant the salvation of the Goddess Anastasia." Faye looked into her coat pocket, and she opened a small bag with a seed in it. She placed the see into the dirt, which was yellow in hue. The seed then dissolved and disappeared into the ground.

"What happened?" Melody asked.

"The seed is now planted in his heart, and he can never be taken over by a demon again unless he rebukes Anastasia and her teachings. The fact that we freed him from the enemy and we planted to see salvation in his mind, he is more likely to live a whole life without fear of ever being possessed again." Percy smiled and put up his thumb as he looked up at the sky. "We should get going then, Faye, if you will."

Faye nodded, and when she put out her hand, a bright light appeared, revealing a door to the child's room. "After you, everyone," Faye said.

Sean, once again amazed by the power of the advanced Dreamweaver, stepped through the door, and he was back in the child's room.

Melody, Percy, and Faye followed and closed the door. They were looking over the child, who had a slight smile on his face.

"Our job is done. Let's go." Percy approached the window and stepped through it, landing on the roof of the house.

Sean looked at the child. He had always been fond of children and often volunteered at homeless shelters. He stopped years ago after people said he touched a child inappropriately. *It was a slip of the hand; he thought to himself, how could they blame me for an accident? No child should ever have to struggle like this.* Sean balled up his fist, and he walked through the window after Melody.

"Let's go home," Percy said.

"How do we get back?" Sean inquired.

"Well, look over there," Percy pointed.

Sean stared across the street toward a bridge. He observed a beam of light, but it was rotating slowly in a whirlwind. It went all the way up into the clouds and into the sky. "What exactly is it?" He inquired.

"It's a spiritual jet stream," Faye said. "Spiritual beings can ride through it. There have been times where demons try to get in there."

Percy nodded in agreeance. "Thankfully, we are covered by the energy from the Goddess Anastasia. So, all of the weaker demons can't harm us. Many of the stronger ones are focused on keeping their strongholds, so most of the time, we don't have to worry about demons trying to reach us, but we must always be cautious and make sure we're not followed. At times jet streams do change rather quick since the balance of spiritual energy flowing throughout the earth is both good and evil."

Stanley L. Garland Jr.

"Let's go." She jumped across the rooftop to the other house. Percy followed, and so did Melody, jumping across 20-foot gaps toward the bridge, which seemed to be two to three miles away.

"Here goes nothing," Sean said. "I feel so alive." Sean ran forward, the moonlight illuminating his way. He jumped over the 20-foot gap with his arms wide open. "Man, this is awesome." He ran forward again, jumped over a 10-foot hole in a 15-foot gap until he reached the others on the other side, and the bridge was right in front of them.

"I feel so alive," Sean said with an enthusiastic tone. "For the first time in a long time, I feel like I'm part of a group. I feel like I have a purpose. It feels right." Sean said, looking at the moonlight.

"Ah, I like what you're saying, but you know that you need to work harder." Faye walked up and punched Sean in the shoulder. "Don't worry, you'll get better, kid."

Percy smiled back at him as he took a giant leap near the edge of the bridge. "Come on, everybody. Sean, you can make it too."

Sean watched the other two jump in front of the home, a 40-foot gap over the water. *I can do this. I can.* Sean closed his eyes right before he opened him. He thought of Tabatha and her love for him. He ran forward, and he crossed the gap, barely making it. Melody caught his hands before he fell back into the water meters below.

"That was a pretty good jump," Melody chirped.

Sean thanked her and looked up at the top of the bridge where the steel bar was connected. It looked like gold dust and energy. It was miraculous to look at. He wanted to stare at it for hours but knew he had to step into it, which was terrifying because it would result in him being dramatically lifted up into the air, which has happened way too many times.

"All right, let's go, y'all," Percy said. Percy ran up the steel bar. He jumped in, followed by Faye and then Melody.

"Here goes nothing," Sean said as he started to run. As he jumped, he felt something pierce his arm. *Aghhh!*

"Sean!" Melody screamed reaching out her hand as the golden whirlwind disappeared up into the sky.

Chapter 12

The trio emerged at the docking station. Melody ran toward Faye, grabbing her tight.

"Sean… we have to go back for him. Something happened. He was attacked; we have to go back." Melody was screaming at the top of her lungs. She grabbed Percy's jacket crying as her tears streamed down her cheeks.

"Slow down," Faye said, "what happened?"

"Sean was just sitting there about to jump in with us, and I saw an arrow pierce his arm, and it went through the metal it was like a light. By the time the words hit my lips, we were up here."

Percy looked over at Melody, his eyes wide open. "We need to get back to him," he said. He broke into a sprint and ran out of the docking station toward the main arena with Faye and Melody close behind.

"Can you get us back to where we came from?" Percy said. "Please, we believe one of our friend is being attacked by we don't know by what, but he didn't make it with us into the funnel back up here."

"Hold on," the woman said, looking into a screen in front of her. "It will be okay. I see where you're at, all right, okay, I can't send you back there, but I can send you twelve miles away. There seems to be another Dreamweaver there in the area. You will arrive in dock 5."

"Close enough, let's go." Percy turned around with the two ladies in tow. They ran into the dock, ready for departure. *Please don't let us be too late.*

Sean turned and looked around, and he saw a woman standing there, but he didn't see where the arrow came from. The woman was slightly bent over and pale. She had a long blade in her right arm. The sword was dripping with blood. She stood there hunched over, looked at him with a slight grin on her face like she was ready to lunge.

Sean's eyes bounced frantically, trying to see where the arrow came from. It was brown in color, but it was shrouded with blood. He pulled it out, looking at the ground where the woman was standing. *I have two options. I think I can run and maybe get gunned by one, or I can fight. It looks like she's about to run. I don't know how long it's gonna take for everybody else to get back. I don't have a weapon, and I can use my fists.* Sean stood there, his legs trembling slightly. His skin had goosebumps as his hair stood up all the way around his body.

He turned around and ran as fast as he could. He leaped off the bridge's apex. Underneath his feet, the steel beams became a blur. He heard the sound of arrows hitting right behind his feet. *I can do this.* Sean continued running till he reached the end of the bridge and went into the forest line. He crouched behind a tree, taking a deep breath and placing his palm on his chest.

Sean leaned on a tree, trying to catch his breath. He stood there looking around at the moonlight, his companion. He glanced up and around to check if another arrow was heading his way. He examined his arm. It was splattered with scarlet blood. I guess mana looks like the blood, he thought, *or maybe it's a sort of combination*. He tried to make himself laugh, but the wound hurt him more than he could comprehend. It felt like it pierced his very soul, like a spirit was screaming in agony.

"That wasn't very nice," a voice said, and he felt the trees splinter behind him.

Sean spun around to see a blade go through the tree and almost miss his skull by an inch. The trees smashed in front of him as he dodged. The lady stooped down, her blade at his chest, laughing hysterically.

Sean reacted quickly, parrying the sword and striking her in the face with his palm. He swung his hand back and landed a second blow to her chin.

"Not bad," the female said, stuttering ever so slightly. "Are you the one who messed up my territory? The demon I sent was slain. The boy, I felt the liberation of the stronghold. How come you're in my environment?" the lady shrieked. She raised her head for a brief period. Her eyes were almost white, with a little black pupil in the center.

"What is your name?" Sean replied as he stood there staring at her attempting to maintain his balance despite his shaky knees.

"I..." the woman said, cackling slightly. "I don't have a name, or do I? It doesn't matter; you can call me Sypher," she said. Her tongue protruded from her mouth, swinging aimlessly.

Sean stood there staring at the woman. *Sypher! What in the world have I gotten myself into?* Sean shook his head. *I didn't get myself into anything. They attacked me. I can't think straight.* Sean began to turn around when he felt another arrow strike his shoulder. *Damn it, that hurt!* Sean resumed his sprint through the woods. He weaved in and out of the tree line, gripping his right shoulder and pulling the arrow out as quickly as he could.

I'm going to die here. His legs felt like they were about to give way. In high school or community college, he was never a runner. He ran the farthest from a blonde girl he kissed in high school after getting the name wrong of the girl who actually liked him.

They're playing with me. They have the ability to murder me at any moment. Or maybe I'm just speedier in this spiritual body. Sean continued sprinting till he reached the end of the tree line and could see a river below him.

He peered out to see the river and more trees on the opposite side. The river was roughly a 10-foot drop in front of him. He wasn't sure his legs could handle the fall, but he knew he had no choice but to leap or get impaled by the nasty woman's sword. Sypher or crazy lady, it didn't matter since Sean didn't want to die.

As he landed in the middle of the river, Sean felt his legs weaken under him. When he turned around, he heard rustling and wind, as well as the sound of death. He was at a loss for what to do.

He struggled across the river to get to the other side. He continued pushing forward, feeling his blood and, worse, his soul suffer since he sensed the presence of the demon energy in his arm. *What will demon blood do to me?* Soaked Sean dragged himself out of the water, his feet trembling with panic. He was racing back to the tree line, unsure of where he was or where he was headed. All he wanted to do was get as far away from the insane lady and the arrows as possible.

Sean looked back, and he saw the woman over the river. She was right behind him. Once again, he was startled by the sound of arrows slicing through the air. *This is how it ends. I am never to see Tabatha or Samantha again.*

"If you want to live, you should get on the ground immediately," a calm voice said.

Sean acted without a second's hesitation. He collapsed to the ground, gasping for air and sobbing at the same time.

The voice was male. The man snapped his fingers, and a bouquet of roses landed in his hand. He drew them all very quick in front of the woman, trying to trap her within its grip. The flowers then bloomed and let off an aura which was very soothing to Sean.

The blade-wielding woman paused just in time to avoid the onslaught. "What are you trying to do to me?" the woman said in a creepy voice. She hunched over, and she looked up over at Sean, "I want him, not you. I want him."

"Then you will have to go through me," the man said. He formed another rose in his hand, and he threw it, striking the woman in the neck.

"My mind," the woman said, "is hurt; my neck is hurt." She started to tremble. "Don't take my meat from me; I need him." The woman turned around, and she began to run off. An arrow fell right in front of the bed of flowers.

Sean turned around and saw a man dressed in all white with a tiny top hat on. His hair was blonde, and his eyes were jade. He had a brown cane with him and sauntered over to where Sean was.

"Oh dear, turn over for me if you will," the man stated.

"Yeah," Sean said as he flipped overlooking up into the man's eyes. Sean noticed three stars on the man's chest and automatically knew he was a Dreamweaver. "Thank you for saving me," Sean murmured.

"What are you doing out here?" the man said in a soft voice. "Well, if you must know, my name is Eric Van Holden. I am a three-star Dreamweaver, as you can probably tell that from observing my outfit. So why is there a no-star out here? The questions keep pilling in my mind," the man said, "but for now, you can gaze upon my beauty." The man stood up, put his hands out, twirling in a circle hugging himself.

The man looked at his watch, and he saw a message. He looked down at Sean and noticed his condition and what he was wearing. "So you were with a group. You are lucky I was around here. I was trying to kill another sypher which is a twin of the one you saw."

"There's another one of those running around? One as creepy and evil as that one? What exactly is a sypher?" Sean tried to sit up, but he felt his body crumble underneath him. All his energy was gone.

"Don't try to move too much," the man said. "I guess I need to carry you. Try not to ruin my clothes," he said, trying to pick up Sean off the ground and putting his arm over him. Eric looked all over Sean's body. "I guess it can't be helped, but I can get these clean when I go back up, but it will not be for a few days. My elegance may be tainted but saving another one of my own is worth the taint." Eric picked up Sean, and put his arm around him.

Sean clinched to the overzealous young man. *I'm a fool. I couldn't even stand against whoever that was. I don't even have a weapon. All I could do was run. How can I even find out what was going on with Samantha if I can't even fight for myself? I have to get stronger; I have to figure out how to control this mana. It would mean to be a spiritual being. I remember what Elijah said; he was talking about my whole body being a spirit. I don't think I thought of Tabatha once. All I thought about was dying; I thought about fear. I must find a way to get back to Tabatha.*

Eric walked over beside the grassy hill next to the bridge. He placed Sean down and sat beside him. "You got pretty banged up," Eric said. "I am surprised you actually survived being at a lower level. Even for someone at my rank, those syphers still cause quite a problem. I was able to kill the other sister, or at least I think I did. I couldn't get confirmation of the body, but I did land a lethal blow to her. Those two sisters run this area. I've been able to get my hands on one but only intel on the other and the lesser demons. I also found out you guys were able to clear out one of the demon's strongholds, and for that, I'm thankful."

Sean thought back to the giant plant that almost killed him. *He calls that a lesser demon.* Thank you for saving me. Thank you for giving me a chance to rest and not die at the hands of the enemy."

"If I didn't defend the weakest among us, what kind of gentleman am I? It's my job to do so. It's the call of the upper ranks to ensure the safety of our little brothers and sisters to make sure they are not killed in the spiritual realm." Eric fluffed his collar sent a kiss into the air.

"Sean!" a female voice rang from the top of the bridge.

Sean watched Melody leap over the bridge and land on the grassy slope where he was lying, to his surprise.

"I'm so happy you're alive." Melody looked at Sean's body up and down. "Oh my goodness! How did you survive?"

"Thank you for not tackling me," Sean said. "It would've hurt really bad if you came and landed on top of me." He looked up, and he saw Faye and Percy coming toward him.

"You're all right, Sean?" Percy said, kneeling down beside him.

"Oh, don't forget about me," Eric said, looking at the active three newcomers who were comforting Sean.

"What is this stiff snob doing here?" Faye said, casting Eric a sassy glance.

"I don't think he is stiff," Sean said, looking up at Eric, who was still sitting on the ground beside him. "He saved me. He made sure I didn't die. All I could do was run."

"You don't know who he is," Percy stated, glaring at Sean. "This is one of the highest Dreamweaver's out there in our society. If he does something good like save your life, you better expect he will be asking for something in return down the road, and he will never let you forget about it."

"What do you mean?" he asked, looking at Percy. "I was helping a fellow Dreamweaver in peril." Eric brushed off his shoulder, narrowing his eyes at Percy. "I expect nothing in return. He is but a little brother to me, and I wanted to make sure he didn't die at the hands of our enemy."

Percy looked up at the sky and then back at Eric. He then put his hand out to the sharp-dressed Dreamweaver. "Thank you for saving our friend."

"Oh, you want to shake my hand," Eric said. "Hold on, let me put my glove on." Eric put on a white glove with feathers on it with an elegant design. He walked over to Percy and put his hand out. "I'm ready now," he said in a soft voice.

The nerve of this fool. Putting a smile on his face, Percy put his hand into Eric's and shook it twice. "Thank you again."

"Don't mention it," Eric said, pulling his hand back, "and like I said, you don't owe me anything. I am happy to see my little brother is still alive. But you would do well to keep track of him. I don't want to have to report your negligence next time. Drink this, it will soothe the pain when they heal you." Eric tossed Sean a small blue bottle that had a happy face on it. "See you." Eric leaped up the grassy hill, and he disappeared into the night.

"Wait, you little!" Faye cliched her fist, starting to make her way up the hill.

"Let him be," Percy said. "We have Sean back. That is what matters most. He needs to be attended to by medical professionals, though, we need to find the nearest jetstream backup." Percy looked back at his watch and noticed the spiritual energy around was relatively low.

"Can demons or whatever those syphers are read this spiritual pressure too?" Sean barely managed to get the words out of his mouth. Melody held him in her lap. *Not a bad view.* Sean glared up at Melody's face.

"We can wait to talk about it," Percy said. "I can't get a read on a jetstream backup. I guess we may have to wait. I don't want to move him too much."

Sean exhausted closed his eyes, and the image he saw in his mind last was Melody's sweet smile.

Chapter 13

Upon waking, Sean glanced across at Melody, who had her hands entwined around his.

She's delightful. He sat there for a moment, not wanting to disturb her sleep. His gaze shifted to the right. It was midnight when he peeked out the window. *How long have I been out? And what happened to that guy? Eric Van Holden was his name. The woman with the bladed hand has a twin. I don't even want to think about what they would do to me.* Sean tried to wake up Melody.

"Huh?" Melody sat up, drool dripping down her mouth and over her cheek. "How long was I asleep?" She quickly wiped the drool off her cheek, embarrassed.

"How long have you been holding my hand?" Sean asked.

Melody blushed; her large bifocals slid slightly on her face. "You have been out for about three days now."

"You've been holding my hand for three days?" Sean said. "Wait, three days; that's a long time, don't you think?"

Melody slid her glasses back toward her forehead. "I've been here this whole entire time to make sure you were healed."

"Three days," Sean almost yelled. "That's a long time, and you were here with me."

"I wanted to make sure you were okay." Melody sighed. "I didn't want you to feel alone. I did hold your hand a lot, though. Touch is essential, especially in the spiritual realm. To touch someone is to feel their soul and mana. It's pretty personal." Melody put her hands to her thighs, shifting her eyes to the left.

Sean's cheeks became scarlet red as he struggled to move his lips.

"Good, you're awake!" Alexis walked through the door with Percy and Faye.

"She took good care of you," Faye said and chuckled. "Good to see you are alive and well. Those demons did a number on you."

"Yes, good to see you as well," Percy said with a big smile. "If you would have died, I don't know what I would have done." Percy came over and put his hand on Sean's shoulder. "You fought well, man."

Sean managed to let go a small smile and then put his hand on Percy's wrist. "Thank you for coming back for me."

"If it wasn't for Eric, you would have been dead by the time we got there." Melody leaned over, putting her hands around Sean, hugging him tightly.

"I am still sore," Sean said, wincing slightly.

"Yes, we can save the pleasantries for later," Alexis said as she walked over to Sean. "I'm glad you didn't laugh when you saw me," Alexis said.

Sean was too exhausted to think back to the trial where Samantha was taken or what they were doing with her. He knew it would be a fool's errand if he even tried to ask Alexis what was going on in front of his friends, so he kept his mouth shut and listened to what she had to say.

"There is an anomaly that has been happening," Alexis said. "These things we call syphers as some sort of demon hybrids. We have yet to discover what they are trying to achieve. What we can tell for certain is that they are our enemies, but we have never seen them with demons."

"Who else can influence such a thing?" Percy looked over at Alexis, who sat in a small brown chair. "I mean, we don't know the full extent of what demons can do either. We're still learning about syphers and their role."

"I agree," Alexis said. "This is where Eric Van Holden has spent the most time, attempting to find out where these creatures originate from. He gave me a full report on the woman you ran into. From what we can gather, they seem to be human. They are humans with demon powers. I would think maybe a sort of demon oversees these abominations."

"The only way to get there is to capture one," Melody said. "We could interrogate it."

"That would work well," Alexis said. "It would seem the only people who have had contact with these so-called syphers are Eric and Sean. So, this is a new development, and we must proceed with caution. These syphers are both a threat to humans and us. Until we can be certain of their power and where they come from I strongly advise not confronting any of them until we know more about their abilities and origins. You're lucky to be alive, young man. I will take my leave now and make sure none of you of this to no one." Alexis turned around and walked out the door, her little legs shuffling as quick as they could.

"Syphers, I wonder what they are truly capable of," Faye said. "It will be interesting to test my strength against one."

"I wonder if we could get one of the upper angels to do it or maybe a five-star Dreamweaver to capture one." Percy put his hands together, and he looked at the ground, his eyes tracing the small squares between the marble floor. "We are being tested with the threat of taking out demons, so if these syphers have similar powers, we have to figure out if they can enter the dream world."

"That would mean we would be going against a direct order from Alexis," Melody stated putting out her arms.

Sean started to think about all the questions running through his mind. All he wanted was to rest. Tabatha, demons, syphers, and Samantha. It was all a bit too much for him to even think about. All he wanted to do was to get well, so he could get back out there and solve each one of the mysteries in front of him one by one. *I don't have any power left.* Looking up at the walls, he saw a blue painting. It reminded him of the ocean waves. The light above him was bright. *I need more rest. I also need a weapon. I need to learn how to harness mana better. So much to do.*

"Sean." Percy walked over to him. "What you experience may cause you to feel worthless. Facing death is often finding out who we really are. Running does not make you a coward. At times running is the best tactic you can use to fight another day."

"There are many exploits of Dreamweaver's who would run away from enemies and disappear. Many of them were beaten and scarred worse than you. Most of them were of higher rank as well." Faye looked at the ground holding her fist together. "We are all trying to get to paradise here, so it would be best if we stuck together."

"Soon, all four of us will go on a mission. I mean," Percy said, "they're usually not that many of us who go out on missions. They should make an exception. Both you and Melody are in training."

"I will go to put in a request," Percy said. "Since I'm a three-star, they should listen to me. It will be days before Sean is ready to go out on another mission. Once you are well, you need to train more. Rest up, Sean." Percy waved as he and Faye walked out the door.

Melody waved back as well, and she turned her eyes to Sean. She took off her glasses and looked at him. "I'm so happy you're okay. I'm going to stay with you. Do you want something to eat? I can order you some soup. It will be good for your throat and warm you up a little bit."

"A cup of coffee will be good with vanilla creamer." Sean smiled, looking over at Melody. "How did you manifest the revolver? You are a pretty good shot with it."

"Thank you," Melody giggled. The young woman walked over to the screen on the wall and pushed two buttons, placing an order for a coffee for Sean. "I have something to tell you."

"What is it?" Sean said, looking over at her.

"It's something that happened in the past. It's a crossroads of sorts. I am standing in the middle, and I make the wrong decision. Here I get another chance to make the right decision. The decision to help others."

"What was the wrong decision?" Sean asked as his eyes trailed across the dark blue walls.

"Here is your coffee," a young man said who was wearing a dark blue suit.

"Thank you," Melody said, grabbing the drinks.

"What did you get?" Sean asked.

"I got an apple cider," Melody said. "It's one of my favorite drinks from my time on Earth."

"I never liked apple cider growing up," Sean said. "It was not my thing, but the smell doesn't bother me too much."

"You're silly," Melody said, and she gently touched his shoulder. "Here is your coffee. Are you able to sit up?"

"Yeah, I think I can." Sean sat up. For the first time since he woke up, he moved his arms and it didn't feel too bad. He twisted his wrists a little bit and flexed his muscles. *I wonder if they healed me with supernatural power. But I guess spiritual healing is a lot different from physical healing. I wonder if my mind got distorted. Now I sound like Elijah.*

Sean took the coffee from Melody, and he sat there sipping it slowly. "Tell me what happened."

"Well, first, you should know I'm thirty-five years old. That is my age in Earth years, but I've been here for quite a while. When I was back on Earth, I lived with a horrible man. It was the type of relationship many people wondered how I even got into. We were together for eight years. When I first met him, he was an amazing gentleman. He would open doors for me. He would drive my car to get it waxed for me and detail it. It was like he was doing everything right."

"Sounds like the perfect gentleman," Sean said.

"Yes, he was almost too perfect, but I didn't trust my intuition. I should have left as soon as I met him, but I chose to marry him after six months of dating him. It was the worst decision I ever made. The first year was beautiful. He did everything right, just like when we were dating, and then the worst happened. He started to beat me. When I spoke out, it seemed as though my words were always wrong. I wanted to take him to church for him to learn about Anastasia's love, and maybe that love could heal his heart. But he thought the love he had for me was enough. He became controlling. He called it love, but it was control."

"Sorry to hear that." Sean lifted his coffee cup, his eyes filled with sorrow. "I've heard horror stories of relationships like that."

"Yeah," Melody said, looking at him. "I took the abuse for several years. I loved him, and I wanted to try to change him, which was foolish. Any counselor will tell you if you're in a relationship like that, you should leave. I eventually managed to help him break through his control and showed him that power is not love. I tried books and counseling. I even worked an extra job for him to get his favorite gift. It was an older car from three generations ago. It took me two years of hard work to be able to afford it. He wrecked it in one week."

"That's pretty rough," Sean said. "He doesn't know what he lost," Sean said gently.

"Yeah. Eight years passed, and I was starting to get really fed up with being mistreated. A restraining order had to be issued against him. When I was sitting in a restaurant with my friends, he walked up to me, violating the order. When my friend said he had no right to approach me, he punched her in the face. I had to run, and I called the police to avoid getting hurt. We were sitting out-side, and I ran around the fence. He caught up to me and grabbed me by the arm, and swung me to the road. I fired three shots into his chest with my handgun. Before I knew it, there were car lights upon me. The next thing I knew, I was here in the Dreamweaver's Society."

"I'm sorry to hear. Sorry you had to kill the man you once loved." *Love I wish....I wish I could go back.* Sean pinched him lips trying to hold back the tears in his eyes.

"It was one of the hardest things I've ever done, but I did it to protect my friends and myself." Melody set her apple cider on the floor and leaned over Sean weeping on his chest. "I'm not fit to be anywhere. I wanted a relationship badly, settled, and my selfishness got me killed. I'm the worst of the worst. I'm a murderer. Is this why I didn't go to paradise? My intentions of finding a relationship were pure. I was trying to find love, and found the worst sort. It's why I work so hard. I pamper myself because I have not been able for a long time."

Sean shifted his coffee from his right to his left hand and caressed Melody's hair. He raised his hand and massaged her head back and forth. "You're not a bad person. We all have those things we struggle with. We are all seeking paradise. All we can do is learn from our mistakes and look forward."

"Thank you! You have a strong heart," Melody said.

"Well, I can't help but feel...you did the right thing....also you are pretty attractive," Sean smirked.

"Thank you for the comfort." Melody lifted her head up, her eyes locked on Sean. She bent and grabbed her apple cider, and took a quick sip.

"So you use your mana in a way to help you look back on the decisions you made. The crossroads where you could have taken a different direction. You draw hope from the situation." Sean took another sip of his coffee.

"Yes, it's painful, but I'm constantly evolving and trying to grow. Maximus, my Guardian Angel, is trying to help me understand my guilt and pain. He said my negative feelings might prevent me from growing as a Dreamweaver. It wasn't until recently that I was able to manifest a pistol. But I think maybe I should shift my focus to the more positive. The past can't change, but like you said, I can learn from it. I have a hard time with it. I have a hard time letting go of the past and looking toward the future. I'm not in paradise, but I have a way to get there, and I need to keep my mind focused."

"I think that's a great idea," Sean said.

"What about you? What are you fighting for?" Melody looked at him, her eyes glowing with care.

I can't tell her about Samantha. I want to make her feel better. I don't want to put my burdens on her. But she shared such intimate details with me about the murder of her husband. I guess I could share a little bit. She is taking the time to get to know me. She cares so much about me even though she has known me for a short amount of time.

"Honestly, I have no memory of what happened to me. I don't know how I died. The night I died, I started to propose to Tabatha. There were loud noises, and that was it."

Melody's eyes perked up, looking at him. "No one has told you anything about how you died? Your Guardian Angel Samantha didn't tell you anything?"

Sean shook his head slowly. "Whenever I tried to ask her, there was something more pressing going on. She told me everything will be revealed in time. I'm still quite confused about it, but I would try not to overthink it. For me, the only way to get through all of this was to keep my mind on Tabatha and concentrate my energies on her."

"Oh, you had a fiancée. I see; that was really amazing that you proposed to her." Melody rubbed her thighs together.

"Yeah, she was an amazing woman. I loved her deeply, and I am trying to figure out what happened. I'm so lost, so she is my focus." Sean tried to hold back the tears. "Hopefully, she got to paradise because she is a better person than me. I'm working hard to get there to see her."

"I hope she's there," Melody said. "Pure love is beautiful." Melody's head tilted to the left. She smiled, looking at Sean. *I shouldn't get in the way of their relationship. I'm pleased that he has a cause to fight for.* "You should get some rest. They said you may be getting discharged in the morning. I'll be here to watch over you."

"Thank you for getting decaf," Sean said. He chuckled and turned over, closing his eyes.

Chapter 14

When Sean awoke, he was startled to find himself back at home. *How did I get here?* He looked around, and he saw Percy resting in the recliner, Melody on the floor, and Faye stretched out beside the bed. *I've always been a loner. Now I have friends. I have real friends, people who care about me.* Sean leaned over to the right, switching to the right side of the bed.

"You can't fool me," Faye said, and she stood up, stretching her arms. "I heard a little creek in the bed. The other two may be knocked out, but I'm awake."

Sean turned back over, and his eyes met Faye, who was sitting up. She was wearing a dark blue sweatshirt. "Good morning," he said to her.

"Good morning to you as well. You look horrible. I'm glad you are feeling better," Faye stated.

"Thanks for the compliment," Sean said, putting his hand through his hair. He felt his head, and around his body, everything from before was healed.

"I don't do this often," Faye said, "but do you want breakfast? I looked through your cabinets, and you have food I can use to make a good meal for all of us."

"It would be great if you made us breakfast, especially after everything that happened," Sean said. "Thank you, and if you want coffee, there's in there as well." Sean smiled as he slammed back into his pillow.

"You know you need to hurry up and rank up so you can get a more prominent place." Faye stood up, and she walked toward the kitchen, where she gently unlocked the cupboards to find the pots and pans she needed to prepare her favorite meal.

"What's all that banging?" Percy mumbled as he sat up. His hair was in disarray as he looked over at Sean, smiling slightly. "Good, you got a whole night's rest. They told us we could move you at night, so we got one of our friends in the taxi service to bring you here, and we did it all without waking you up."

"Yeah," Melody said softly as she curled up underneath the blanket. "We couldn't leave you by yourself. I was with you, but the other two wanted to make sure you are okay as well."

Sean had to go underneath the blanket for a moment as he felt tears well up into his eyes. He had a group of people who genuinely cared about him. *Do you see this, Tabatha? I have people; I have friends. People who care about me. You always said I should put myself out there more. I'm trying to. I wish you could see this as well, Samantha. I'm going to figure out what's going on.*

"Good you're all awake," said Percy.

Faye looked back her finger pointing furiously at her friends. "Make the coffee, Melody. Percy, you come over here to help me cook."

"All right, all right," Percy said. "I'm getting up. I'm going to wash my face."

"All right, Sean, you do nothing. You sit there and relax." Faye looked back at him with a stern glance as she started to stir flour in a bowl with milk.

I don't know whether to be terrified or thankful. Sean snuggled underneath the blanket as he watched Percy, Melody, and Faye get to work.

"No, that's too much," Faye said. "Pour half a cup of water and half a cup of almond milk. Let me do it. You can go over and put all the coffee cups on the table."

She is really driving them hard. Sean wrapped himself in the blanket, his gaze shifted between his new found friends. *She is doing all this for me. It's nice to see a different side of her.*

The sizzling pancake aroma filled the room. There were smells of blueberry, strawberry banana, and fresh syrup Faye made.

"All right now, you can get out of bed," Faye said. "The coffee is made, and the pancakes are done. You better like them! I put my heart and soul into them. This is my grandmother's recipe, so if you don't like him, you will make my grandmother cry, and my grandmother is probably in paradise. So don't make her cry, all right?" Faye leaned forward tapping her right foot on the ground turning her lips towards the ceiling.

Melody, Faye, and Sean let out a slight laugh as they all proceeded to the table.

"I'm going to miss this," Melody said. "We are thankful you are alive, Sean. We're grateful you're here. We are grateful you have a second chance."

Percy put his fork down, his eyes cutting toward Sean. "Moving forward, it will be the four of us. I had a conversation with Alexis, and she feels something is stirring. She wants me to keep an eye on you, and I didn't object."

"Since Percy and I are a team, I'm coming along as well," Faye stated. She took a sip of her coffee as she twirled her hair. "You better not fall behind. We're going to make sure you are trained up."

"I promise I will not fall behind," Sean said, taking a bite of the buttermilk pancake with blueberries on top of them. *This is amazing!* "Faye, this is so delicious," Sean said, talking with food in his mouth. "I hope your grandmother is crying for a good reason, because these flavors are on point."

"I told you, you can't beat generational pancakes. I don't overeat because we're going to go train today." Faye let go a slight giggle as she looked over at Percy.

Percy sat with his elbows on the table and his hands interlocked. "Don't worry, we are not going to push you too hard. We do have to go over this. We need to figure out what type of weapon you can manifest. Sorry, do you even have the power to manifest a weapon? I took the time to speak with Elijah about your spiritual potential, and it seems you have the overwhelming will to help others. He also said you can be guarded at times."

Sean nodded as he took another bite of his pancake, barely taking the chance to swallow.

"I guess you haven't had a good meal in a while," Melody stated. "I've had one meal from Faye before, but it was like sandwiches, and it was perfect. It was more of a snack, but now to see her cook like this, I'm glad she's going to be with us."

"It's okay to be guarded," Faye said. "It took a while for me to trust Percy. I thought Percy was an arrogant prick most of the time. Over time I've discovered that he actually cares about people."

Percy chuckled, laying back in his chair. "Remember when I tried to pick up a pencil for you the first day I met you? You slugged me to the face because you thought I was copping a glance."

"I was wearing a tank top that day, and I didn't know you. You have to forgive me." Faye let out a loud laugh as she slapped the table. "I will never forget that day."

"How long ago was that?" Sean inquired.

"It was about two years ago in human time," Percy stated.

"Can I ask you something?" Sean asked. "I haven't had a chance to read the rulebook all the way through, but I do remember reading there are certain ranks that come with specific perks. Is that correct?"

"Yes, you are correct," Faye said. "The ranks go from one to five stars. The more dreams you go into and demons you kill, the higher up you go."

"It's so much more than that," Percy said. "You have people who have killed many demons who are still emotionally immature to receive even a one-star rank. Alexis keeps tabs on every Dreamweaver. We also have to file reports on what we see and any collateral damage to the humans we interact with."

"Collateral damage," Sean inquired.

Faye sighed stirring her coffee. "Yes, when we don't kill a demon, it makes it harder to access their dreamscape the second time around. There are situations when we fail even after a second attempt..."

"Then the person is doomed," Melody asks.

"The outlook would be bleak, and at times they die. We want humans to live a whole life while they are on Earth. That sort of existence is not one worth having. Sorry to get somber," Percy said as he took a sip from his coffee.

"From what I read in the book, there are lower ranks as well." Melody had a big smile on her face as she took another bite of the pancakes.

"You're correct," Faye stated. "There are three lower ranks. Those underclasses are presented in the form of bronze bars. So underclass one, two, three."

"When will I know I'm ready for a rank?" Sean stared at Percy, awaiting an answer. His eyes were slanted as if he knew it would take a long time.

"You will be presented with an under rank when your superiors feel you are ready to take on more complex cases. The dream we entered the other day was a bit of an anomaly. It was ranked 2.2 out of 10, but the demon in there was rated a 5.5 when it should've been three or four. Since Faye and I are now your superiors, we will put a request for your promotion when we feel you are ready. Since we're friends, don't think we're not going to judge you harshly. If we don't train you properly and if we rank you up too quickly, it will lead to a swift death in the dreamscape."

Sean let go a nervous laugh. "I guess you were buttering me up, Faye, for the pain that was coming."

"You are quick one to catch on," Faye said, winking at him and letting out a short giggle. "I guess I also actually wanted to cook a meal for you. It's good to have a routine and a team that takes care of each other. So, with that being said, prepare for the pain because it's coming. I'm not going to take it easy on you. Percy is a softy but not me," she said with a big smile. She placed her hands on the table and rested them there.

Sean stopped chewing his pancakes for a moment, and he let go of a slight laugh. "Now I am scared." Sean giggled, and the others joined in for a round of laughter.

The minutes pass as they enjoy their meal and start to clean up the dishes.

"All right, everyone, your food should be digested by now. We were going to head to the training grounds here in about ten minutes. I bought clothes for everyone to change into," Percy said.

The group of four finished each of their tasks as all of them went into the restroom one after another to change into their clothes.

Sean was the last to go in to change. He opened the small box, and he noticed a pair of matching shorts and a top blue in color. It had the number '01' on it and the word 'trainee' on the bottom. Sean looked at the bottom of the boxes, and he found a small letter of sorts. *Look at this.* He pulled up the letter, and he opened it.

I will always be near your heart because those who are near in spirit no distance can separate.

Sean felt his knees buckle, and the letter fell from his hand, hitting the floor. He noticed it had the letter T written in cursive. *It can't be. It can't be! This is what Tabatha always said before she went on her business trips.* Sean put his hand over his mouth, and he felt his body almost go numb. *This letter must be from her. This can't be a sick joke. This has to be from her. She knows where I am. But I don't know what happened to her.* Sean sat there leaning on the wall. He felt like he would throw up, but he also felt like he was about to cry. *Okay, focus, Sean.*

"You okay in there?" Melody asked as she knocked on the door gently.

"Yeah, I'm okay," Sean said.

"Well, meet you outside," Melody said.

Sean put the letter inside a box, closed it, and put it underneath the bathroom sink. *Tabatha, if you're near, please let me know where you are.* Sean felt his heart swell up with emotion as he grabbed the door handle and walked out the door.

Chapter 15

Sean walked out of the front door to see Melody on her broom and Percy with a type of scooter.

"Have you ever been in the air scooter?" Percy inquired.

"I never even knew it existed," Sean observed the scooter. It was yellow in color with black stripes on the side. It had one wheel in the front and two in the back. The seat was like plush brown leather. The backseat matched the front one as well.

"Come on, hop on," Percy said as he waved his hand, directing Sean toward the seat behind him.

Never a dull moment here. Sean walked over to the backseat. *I better put the seatbelt on. Never can be too safe.*

Melody peered over at Sean with rosy cheeks. Faye was sitting on the backside of her broom, clutching Melody tight.

"The training grounds are behind the housing unit. We could walk there, but I always like a good flight," Percy said. The old scooter lifted into the air with no sound. Suddenly, it burst into lighting speed, and it did a flip into the air. Sean's lips once again blistered.

Surprised I haven't coughed up my food yet. Sean held onto the back of Percy's seat with a death grip.

"I pushed it up to fifteen on the speed gauge," he said as he went up into the clouds and then dropped back down at lighting speed. Percy smiled as he waved up to the scooter, and it made a loud noise.

Before he knew it, Sean was staring at a vast green field littered with people.

The scooter came to a halt, and it trickled down slowly on the edge of the field. Sean scanned the field with littered with scooters, two dragons sleeping, and other brooms.

"Pretty fun, wasn't it?" Percy said.

Fun wasn't isn't the first word that came to my mind "I think I'm okay. The pancakes almost came up," Sean stated with a slight giggle.

Percy put his hand on Sean's shoulder. "I'm glad you didn't throw up."

Sean looked intently at Percy, his eyes squinted slightly from the sun.

Melody guided her broom beside him. She did a slight twirl, parking it sideways.

"Not too bad," Faye said. "You could have pushed it a bit more. I live for speed," she yelled.

"I didn't know you like speed. Next time I have to make it a bit faster," Melody said with a slight giggle.

Melody approached Sean, and Percy gave them a nod. They moved over to the grass and found an open area.

"Sean, you are going to work on hand-to-hand combat with me," Percy stated. "I will be training with you for a little, and then we will switch over to Faye and back and forth with you two. Melody, since you are a bit farther along than Sean, you will be training first, and then you will switch over to me."

Melody nodded, and she walked away with Faye about forty feet from where Sean was standing.

"All right, Sean, the first thing you need to know is demons come in different varieties. You can specialize in distance magic, up-close magic, hand-to-hand combat, and weapons. You must understand and master the encounters with each one of these situations. We will be a team, but most Dreamweaver's are sent into these situations alone. I am thankful I will be accompanying you."

"I am thankful for this as well. What you are talking about is mind-boggling. The only thing I could think about was running away the other day." Sean leaned back and stretched, his back twitching slightly. *I'm still not 100 percent.*

"Sean, you're doing too much thinking and too little feeling," Percy stated, pacing around the novice trainee. "Remember, we are in the spiritual realm now. When you were back on Earth, all you had was your intellect. Try to focus more on the spirit. You need to focus on the fluidity of your movements. Now try to punch me, okay?"

Spirit! I've been thinking a lot, especially about what happened with Tabatha. I wonder if she's here or if she wrote to me from Paradise. I can barely concentrate. "All right, here I come," Sean yelled. His feet dug into the ground sprinting forward, his right fist barreled toward Percy's chest.

Percy observed his movements, took a step to the left, and slammed his palm into Sean's chest.

Sean landed hard on his knees and turned over on his back, breathing heavily. "No fair, you've done this for a long time."

"You're new, so it's easy to beat you up. I don't take pleasure in it. Faye may take pleasure, but I'm trying to show you how to be better. What did you do wrong?" Percy asked.

"I don't know. I ran toward you," Sean stated, his eyes bouncing around, looking up at the sun and back toward Percy.

"You have to learn to first observe your enemy's weakness. Think back to the giant plant that almost ate you." Percy started to walk in a counterclockwise motion around Sean.

Sean's eyes tried to trace what Percy was doing by keeping up but felt as if he was lost.

"The monster that almost killed you had a lot of weak points. It couldn't look up because its head was slumped over. So the whole time it was looking at you, Faye saw an advantage, and she delivered a kick that knocked it out. Then I came up with my blade from underneath, providing the death blow."

"I see," Sean said, turning to keep up with Percy once again. In an instant, he delivered a false kick to Percy's ankle. Percy jumped back as Sean tackled him.

"Excellent idea to use a diversion. What do you do next? How are you going to follow up? The demon would've already stabbed you by now or done something worse. Don't hesitate!" Percy bellowed as he put his arm down on Sean's neck.

Sean took his fist, cocked it back, and punched it toward Percy's face.

Percy shifted his weight from the tackle, standing up and dodging the punch. "It was an excellent instinct to come to this point, but once again, this is training, and you had time to react. Your movements have to be almost cerebral," Percy said. "You have to be able to act at a moment's notice."

Sean nodded, wiping the sweat off his head. *I have to get better.* He started running, and he let go of his anger. He punched, getting back and forth again, pushing his spiritual muscles and his physical muscles more than ever before.

Percy dodged to the left and then to the right. "Good, keep punching. You have to work these muscles."

Sean paused his blows and delivered an uppercut to Percy's chin with his right hand.

"Nice switch up, but again too slow on the defense." Percy took his elbow and slammed it into Sean's stomach.

Sean bent over and grabbed his chest in anguish, putting his hand out to the sun.

"That's pretty good," Percy said. "You got me to work up a sweat, man." Percy walked over, putting his hand out as he put it out toward Sean.

I got him. Sean leaped up and clenched his fist toward the jaw of Percy.

Percy did not react; he took the blow in full force, and he fell back on the ground. "Not bad. At times you must be less than honorable when you're dealing with demons. Our goal is paradise, but monsters will show you no mercy. Good job!"

"Thank you," Sean said. *Oh, that hurt!* Sean took his other hand and nursed his right fist.

"You have bruises. Thankfully you heal a bit quicker since you're in the spiritual realm. Your body right now is a combination of your Earth body and your spiritual mana. You recover quickly after, but you also feel the pain. All part of the job," Percy said.

"I appreciate your training. I'm going to keep pushing myself," Sean affirmed.

Percy nodded as he shifted his gaze to Melody and Faye, who were engrossed in a training exercise.

Melody snapped her fingers, and her pistol disappeared suddenly. Faye grinned as she placed her hand on Melody's shoulder.

"All right, who's up next?" Faye said as she walked over, smiling at Sean. "All right, let's go," she bellowed. She took him away from Percy, who put his hands up, struggling slightly.

"Good luck, Melody," Sean yelled as he waved at her.

Melody nodded and cast a glance. "You know what to expect with Faye."

Sean knew in his spirit the next hour of his life would be the worst.

"All right, ten push-ups now," Faye yelled, pointing toward the ground.

Sean could barely catch a break. He found himself in a push-up position going up and down with Faye.

"We are doing five sets of ten, which means fifty. Don't fall behind," Faye aired.

Sean nodded as he pushed his upper body as fast as he could. *This is a bit harsh after the past few days' events.* To get stronger and not die in a battle with syphers or demons he needed to push himself. He pushed up and repeated until he found himself out of breath. His thoughts about Tabatha and the hope of seeing her soon. He pushed out again. Fifty push-ups later, he thought about giving up.

"Good, now that we are nice and warmed up, we're going to work on grappling. After grappling, we are going to manifest a weapon or see if you can."

Warmed up! This woman is crazy. Sean nodded without thinking. "What are we going to do first?" he asked her.

"We're going to focus on a headlock. This is how you do it. I am going to walk behind you, and I will then interlock my arms and then wrap them around your neck."

Sean felt the pressure of the hold. *Man, she is strong.*

"Now try to escape free of this grasp," Faye replied.

Sean squeezes to the left and then to the right. It felt like a strong hold, so he leaned forward but felt his feet buckle slightly. The world around him was spinning.

"That was pathetic." Faye let go of the grip and turned around to look at Sean. "You have no grappling skills whatsoever, so you've never wrestled when you were a kid. You never did any wrestling in high school." Faye looked at him tapping her foot. "We got a lot of work to do," she said. "You never know what type of tools you may need when you're fighting a demon. Now we also have this new threat upon us. We have no idea what the limits of your skills are, so you have to understand each move you make is vital."

"I will try my best, and I'm still getting used to this body," Sean said. "I mean, I didn't work these muscles at all when I was on Earth, much less now that I need to understand mana and how to work spiritual muscles." Sean's chest was heaving, and his hair was wet from the exertion.

"All right now, put me in the same headlock. Lock your arms and put them around my neck." Faye put her arms by her side as she stood there with her eyes closed.

Is it all right to make it so tight? The pancakes were great. Sean approached and wrapped his arms around her neck.

Faye moved in a moments notice, tackling Sean to the ground and putting him in an armbar in an instant.

Sean fell to the ground screaming in pain.

Faye jumped up with a smile on her face, and she bowed to him gently. "That was pretty bad. Any idea how I countered your headlock so quick?"

"You hit me with your big butt," Sean said. "I mean, it is pretty curvy, don't you think?"

"I will pretend I didn't hear that," Faye said. "Yes, I did use the weight of my backside to pin you down and put you into an armbar."

"That hurt pretty bad," Sean rubbed his arm gently.

"We need to work on the stamina of your legs. I don't want to push you too hard, maybe I did already, but you need to learn. You're under my and Percy's watch now. Take it seriously, or you will die. If you die, it will not set me back from getting to paradise, but I don't want to lose a teammate. I won't be making pancakes for you to make you feel better."

"They were pretty good," Sean vocalized.

"Oh hell yeah, they were. Our centuries-old recipe never goes out of style. One day I hope my daughter will make it as well."

"Your daughter," Sean inquired.

"It's nothing! Let's work on manifesting weapons." Faye put out her hand. Her arm became engulfed in a green vortex of energy, and a blade appeared in her palm.

Sean's eyes traced the blade, which was black in color.

This is so cool. The blade had what appeared to be lightning bolts surrounding it.

"Here, catch this," Faye said. She nonchalantly threw the blade toward Sean.

Sean put his hand out gripping the hilt of the blade, and immediately, his whole body slammed to the ground. *Oh my gosh, it's so heavy. She was holding it like it was a paper airplane.* One of Sean's hands was wrapped around the hilt as he struggled to lift it. The blade barely lifted off the ground. *I can do this!* While perspiration dripped down his palms and all over his body, he clutched the steel firmly in both his hands.

"Not bad, that's actually a level III ranked heaven weapon. Over time, Dreamweaver's can learn the skill of manifesting weapons. As you see, Melody can create a revolver. Percy can manifest a sword. My talents are different. I can manifest several different weapons though I choose to use my fist and my legs because I feel most connected that way when I fight. I have a variety of weaponry at my disposal in case I find myself in a tight spot. It took me twenty hours of concentration in the Waterfall of Enlightenment to manifest this. The water was so cold it even touched my soul."

"This is scary," Sean said. He could not utter any more words out of his mouth as he concentrated on holding the blade. He felt the edge start to slip, and he gripped it again.

"Hold up. I'm interested to see how your stamina will hold out holding a powerful weapon. How does your mana feel?" She looked at Sean, curious.

"I'm thinking about my fiancée. This is how I'm holding the weapon." Sean closed his eyes for a moment. "My body feels like it's about to explode. Guess this is what you called the spirit. It's like a rush or a wave of energy I can't comprehend. I don't know how to explain it. It's like this weapon draws from it, but I can't move the blade at all."

"A spiritual weapon requires you to channel your mana flow," she said. "You will need to build strength to use a weapon like this right off the bat, but at some point, you will understand how to master the technique of mana flow whatever weapon you want. Yet you need to connect to your spirit. There is no certainty that connecting to your spirit will lead to the creation of a weapon. In doing so, you will see the best results in your training and what accounts for the dreamscape. You can let it go now."

Sean collapsed to the ground, gasping for breath as he lost control of the sword. Almost as if he was about to pass out or was on a kind of high, his body felt heavy. *This is mana flow. If I can learn how to harness this, maybe if I breathe more and focus on Tabatha a bit more, I can use weapons. I can manifest weapons.*

Faye snapped her fingers as the blade vanished and green light poured back into Faye's own body.

Sean laid on his back, looking up at the sun. "I have a question for you, Faye."

"Go ahead, shoot," she said.

"When you fight, are you channeling your mana? Is it your own raw strength?" Sean wiped his head, looking at the brazen woman.

"I will say it is a little bit of both. You won't believe this, but I was like an accountant back on Earth. I ran an online fitness blog focused on kickbox and aerobic workouts. So naturally, I have strong muscles, but the mana also helps when fighting the demons. I channel a specific amount of mana when I'm punching, so if a monster is powerful, then I'm going to go all out. But if it's more of a demon on the scale of 2.3 or 2.5, then use the appropriate amount of mana I need to not wear myself out."

"You were an accountant," Sean questioned.

"Were you even listening about the mana flow?" Faye said.

"Yes, I was. I did hear about the punch and everything you mentioned. I can't imagine you working with numbers. You seem so intense," Sean stated.

"Numbers are intense, especially if you budget for a large company," Faye laughed. "Never judge a book by its cover. Last lesson for today." She closed her eyes and put out her hand, and snapped her feet.

Sean looked at her hand, and he saw she was holding a small knife.

She then placed the knife in Sean's hand. "Try this."

Sean took the knife, and he felt his hands immediately fall toward the ground. *I can do this.* He lifted his hands up, and he gripped the knife in one hand. He turned it over and looked at the hilt. He noticed the figure of a dragon with his mouth open again on the hilt. It was breathing fire, pointing toward the blade.

"Go ahead and swing it around. I want to see what you got." Faye sat on the ground with her arms folded, staring up at Sean.

"All right, here goes nothing," he bellowed. Sean took the knife, and he swung it forward, striking it as a ball of flame came out of it. *Oh my gosh.* The ball of flame trickled out then disappeared out of thin air. "What happened?" he asked Faye.

"Your blade, or I shall say knife, has a magical limit on it, like a magic knife shooting flames. You didn't feel any heat, though. When you held the blade, did you," she stated.

"No, I didn't feel any heat at all; I swung it, and a fireball came out, and I could have hit the woman over there. I was terrified I was going to hurt her," Sean said.

"It's good to see you can handle weaker weapons. You saw the danger of hurting someone else and limited the range subconsciously. That is some amazing skill for a novice. This is a junior-level blade. I'm proud of you," Faye said, clapping her hands.

Sean smacked his hands on his cheeks. "I think I have had enough. I'm rather tired."

"Fair enough, I pushed you pretty hard," Faye said. Suddenly, the knife vanished from Sean's hand and returned to hers as she moved closer to Sean.

"How long did it take you to manifest this?" Sean started to walk back toward Percy and Melody.

"I will say I took a few months to manifest the knife. The first time, I was on a mission with a more experienced Dreamweaver, and he died saving me. I barely got out alive," Faye stated solemnly.

"I'm sorry to hear," he said. "What was his name?" Sean asked.

Before Faye could get the words out of her mouth, Percy ran up and greeted them.

"It's been a few hours," Percy said. "How's everybody feeling? I had a pretty good workout. And while we were over here, I got notified of a mission. Tomorrow at 8 a.m. Everyone get some rest, and we will meet up at the upper docks." Percy waved, and Faye walked off with him.

Sean waved to the two higher rank Dreamweaver's.

"How did everything go?" Melody put her arm on her shoulder and smiled at him. "Are you sore from all the training with Faye?"

"Yea! She gave me this spiritual weapon which was crazy. It made me feel powerful, but I couldn't even move with it. It took all of my energy to hold it." Sean rubbed his biceps, thinking about the training Faye put him through.

"Make sure you soak in water tonight because you are going to be sore for tomorrow's mission." Melody put her hands behind her as she leaned forward, winking at him. "Oh no!"

Sean leaned, catching her glasses before they hit the grass. "Here you go."

"Thank you," she said, rubbing them off with her shirt. "I need to get going. You know I am worried about tomorrow's mission. With those syphers running around, we don't know where their allegiance lies. Are they separate or with the demons? Either way, the most important thing to do is be prepared." Melody waved, and she walked away.

Sean looked up at the afternoon sun. I forgot to smell the letter to see if it had her scent. He walked up toward the stairs, which led to a main walking area off the field.

Chapter 16

Sean glared around the room, holding his head. The clock on the wall said 7 a.m. *I guess I need to get ready. There was something in my dream. There was something about a wine bottle, and I thought I felt this hard sensation on the back of my head. Somebody hit me, man I can't remember. I remember Tabatha screaming she would marry me. She said yes, and then darkness.*

Sean looked over at the counter beside him. He pulled the letter from the drawer, and it had Tabatha's name on it. He took a quick look at it, and it reminded him of her. *She has to be in paradise. She has to be. There is no other way around it. I can't deny it smells like her. It had her scent. Smells like the first time we kissed. The first time we made out and had sex together. The intimacy was so sweet. I have been given a second chance, and I can't waste it. I can't procrastinate anymore; I have to do better.*

Sean sat up and put the letter back on the shelf. *Eventually, I'm going to have to bring someone into this. There is much more to this story; I need to watch my back. There's so much I don't understand.* While his coffee was brewing, Sean walked over to the closet and pulled out a white-& blue suit. It had his initials on the front and a rose tucked in it.

Looks like I'm going to be fancy today. These custom suits are on point! I like that it fits my body, but it's not so tight that I can't move. Sean walks over to the bathroom in the other room to wash his face. I've never done this before if I guess it's time to say a prayer.

"Goddess, please bring my beloved Tabatha back to me if you can hear my prayer. I'm going to work hard no matter how long it takes to get her back into my arms. Please listen to me, help me be a better man. Amen."

Most people pray with their eyes closed, but Sean couldn't close his eyes, for he was too preoccupied with the thought of seeing his love. He splashed hot water over his face and went back to the kitchen. This time he made French vanilla instead of regular vanilla.

He popped a little cinnamon on top, completing his masterpiece. Mixing up a bowl of grits and cheddar cheese, he scarfed it quick as he looked up at the clock and saw it was 7:45.

"Sean, are you there," a voice called out from the door.

"Yeah, hold on, I'm coming, Melody." Sean walked up to the door, opened it, and the cheerful woman stepped in, closing the door behind her.

"Our second mission is today," she said, walking in and taking place on the sofa. "Are you nervous?" Melody stretched out, letting out a giant yawn.

Sean looks at Melody, who is dressed in a pink outfit with black leggings. She wore her hair in pigtails with a bow at the base, all the way to her ankles.

"You really let your hair go for this one. Also, yeah, I'm a little nervous." Sean took another sip of his coffee and walked toward her.

"Before we go to, I'm going to tie my hair up a little bit. But I wanted to really go all out with the outfit. Plus, you know pink is my favorite color. Have you checked your bank account lately?"

"Oh yeah, that's right, I can access it from my watch, right?" Sean tapped his watch twice, and he saw a small gold card pop up. The gold card had a smiley face on it, and it bounced around a little bit as it showed a balance of 20k gold. "I got 20k Gold."

Melody let go a slight sigh as she looked at Sean, smiling a little bit. "That's not a whole lot of money," she said to him. "That may get you a few meals or a new outfit if you want one. Some people here really like to go all out with their fashion, and there are excellent boutiques if you like to go shopping. I met a fashionista, and I have a friend who enjoys dressing up when she wants to fight. People call her the elegant warrior."

"Elegant warrior," Sean said. *That sounds like a superhero name. Everything here is supernatural, so I guess hero names, just like Dreamweaver names, sound normal.* "People like her?"

Using her index finger, Melody touched her chin, humming a little bit. "It's safe to say she has haters. She also has a group of people she confides in. She's a little smug and a little rough around the edges. Her demon-killing tactics are rather cruel. I haven't seen her in a while, but occasionally we sip tea together and reminisce about our lives in the past. I guess today, I draw my fashion inspiration from her. You almost ready?"

Sean nodded, and they walked out of the door. In the back of his pocket, the letter from Tabatha was neatly placed. Maybe this is sort of a spiritual connection. *Perhaps I can draw from its power to manifest weapons since I have an item with her scent. Who knows, the possibilities could be endless, and I still don't know what weapon I want to use in a fight or how to channel my mana fully.*

Melody hopped on the broom and Sean put his arms around her. The ride was casual today. Sean looked out at the beautiful scenery. In the distance he could see what seemed to be a home with a stream flowing from it, and he spied it from a distance. So far away yet so near at the same time. It was like they were supposed to go there, but the next moment it disappeared from his eyes. Sean was lost in thought as they landed at the station to be transported to Earth.

"You are awful quiet," Melody said as she flew the broom into a locking mechanism on the dock.

"I was thinking about my girlfriend. I saw something on the mountain, and it intrigued me. Maybe I can visit it someday." Sean talked of his love of Tabatha to Melody as they checked into the dock station.

The cheerful woman pointed to the door toward dock station six.

Sean followed Samantha down the busy hallway toward dock 6. "There is so much I have yet to experience here in the

Dreamweaver Society. To me, it's almost like a bit of heaven or par-adise. You can get quite comfortable here. Why not just chill here? I heard people have been here for over 100 human years, still trying to work their way into paradise."

Melody nodded her head, looking back at him. "The God-dess Anastasia wants the purest people in paradise."

Sean scratched his head and took a small sip of his coffee. "I guess it makes sense people stay here. Maybe they feel they don't deserve to be there."

"That's interesting. I never thought about it that way. It could be guilt that keeps people here. Maybe there is no one up there waiting for them. They would be alone. I think Tabatha is up there for you." Melody twirling around walking backwards winking at him.

Sean nodded and smiled at Melody. They turned the corner and went into dock station six.

"You're one minute late," Faye said, crossing her legs. "We need to get going. But because we have to wait five minutes and get ready to tell you what's going on, take a seat to enjoy your cof-fee. Next time whoever may be too late, probably Sean, will get one less pancake," she said, putting her hand on her knee.

Sean wiped his mouth, and he looked over at Melody.

Percy was flipping through the holographic screen in front of the room. "This is our assignment today. Meet Richard Waller, watchmaker extraordinaire: He's one of the best. Despite the hopes of many, his wife succumbed to cancer, and he was unable to complete his magnum opus."

"How tragic," Melody gasped, putting her hands together, looking at the picture of the old man with a receding hairline.

Percy clicked off the screen, his face stern with determination. "Tragic indeed. I hope you two got enough rest."

Melody and Shawn nodded.

"The pink looks good on you," Faye said, looking at the outfit from top to bottom.

"Thank you," Melody stated, twirling in a circle putting her fist into the air.

"We are running a bit late, so let's get going. The demonic pressure will be a bit higher this time. Focus and breathe when we get there. Remember, each situation will present its own challenges." Percy looked stern at Sean, then all of a sudden, they were gliding toward Earth, a modest cottage in the mountains coming to their viewpoint.

The group of four landed on the ground gently. The darkness was darker than normal.

Sean glared up at the numerous stars and then down at the classic cars down the street. The smell was of honeysuckle and dew.

"Prepare your mind for demonic pressure," Percy said.

"You look distracted, Sean," Faye stated, looking back at him, "you need to keep your head in the game."

"How did you know?" Sean said. They went through the brown door of the house without making a sound.

"A woman knows," Faye uttered. She giggled and turned around, looking Sean up shaking her head.

"Don't try to understand women," Percy verbalized. "It will leave you stranded and alone on an island."

Ain't that the truth. Sean shifted his gaze across the walls. Clocks of different shapes and sizes decorated the walls of the home, and a photograph of a family hung on one of them. It was a family of six, with four children and their parents. It would appear the children have long since gone and left home. But there were still toys scattered around, maybe implying there were grandchildren that would come about. It smelled of old coffee beans. *I like that smell.*

Turning the corner, he saw Percy and Melody, and he stared at all the oversized chairs. Before him, he saw a man slightly overweight, in blue overalls, drool dripping on his face.

Faye's foot beat rhythmically. "This is the guy. Looks like he's sleeping in his overalls after eating soggy cereal. The cereal isn't even name brand. What a shame," Faye affirmed a disgusted look planted on her face.

Percy looked over at her, trying not to laugh, and nodded. "All right, everybody, hold on and grab onto each other."

Sean closed his eyes, holding on to Melody. He felt his body go numb for a second, and he planted his feet and breathed deeply.

He was able to move his right hand, pressed the watch, and looked at the demonic pressure. *Level three, that's not bad.* He kept breathing and began to move.

"Got the hang of it," Faye said, looking at Sean and Melody.

"I'm getting better," Melody said, wiping her head of a little bit of sweat. "It's still hard to do. This is the second time we've entered a dream."

"One more reason to stay focused and take care of business," Percy said with a slight smile. "You ready to go back there, Sean?"

"Yeah, I'm ready," Sean said as he stood up straight with a wide grin on his face. *You're in my mind, Tabatha. I love you, baby.*

Sean's eyes traced to a tall set of stairs in front of them. There were no elevators around, to his dismay. The stairs were brown in color. Depending on the hue, they seemed to be anything from tattered and shabby to immaculate. Some stairs were faded going up, others looked like they were about to give in, and you could fall to your death.

Melody looked over the platform. She felt the gray silver bar that would protect them was cold to the touch. "Guys, over here," she said. She wiped her oversized bifocals. It was pitch-black, but she could see faces all around her.

"Get back," Percy said.

Melody fell back, and one of the black shadow faces lunged up.

Percy ran forward, manifested his sword, and he sliced the sizable black face in half. It was pure darkness.

"Thank you," Melody said, scurrying back to the center of the platform.

The brown boards they were standing on were creaky. The walkways ahead of them were lighted by a great pillar of light that emerged from the top of the steps.

"We need to get moving," Percy said. "The demons have a strong presence and are attacking us. We need to go." Percy put his sword beside him with a stern look on his face looking back at Faye.

Melody and Sean nodded and followed the two more experienced Dreamweaver's to the first flight of stairs.

"Have you seen anything like this before," Sean said, looking up at Percy and Faye. "What do those things want from us?"

"Probably your soul," Faye said with a slight giggle.

"Why did it look like that," Sean inquired, "but really, what was that?"

"Honestly, I don't know what that was," Percy proclaimed. "I've never seen anything like it. The dreamscape is endless, we do not know everything, and the human mind can manifest almost anything. This is why you always have to be prepared and react."

Sean thought back to the angels and their courses. He thought about the mental tests to spiritual and physical stamina, and of all he went through to get to where he is now. Though it was brief, those intense few hours with each of his masters made sense now.

"I understand," Sean affirmed, nodding. "You doing okay, Melody?"

Melody looked back. "Yeah, I'm okay." She darted upstairs; she ran past Faye, looking out at the infinite darkness around them. "What does all this mean? The lights illuminate only these stairs," Melody said.

Percy turned a corner, and he said, "Forty flights of stairs, and I am feeling fatigued. The demonic pressure went up to 3.5. Hold on, everybody." He looked back at the faces below them in the darkness.

With widening eyes, Faye twisted her body and smacked her foot into one of the demon's faces. "The stairs are sinking into the darkness. We have to go," Faye yelled.

Sean looked back, and he saw nothing but darkness below them. He ran upstairs, gripping the bars. Percy and Faye sliced and kicked away at the faces that were coming at them.

"Give up! Your girlfriend hates you and is with another man," the face hissed. His hands gleamed emerald green as he crashed his right fist into the creature's face, disintegrating it. *I guess I can fight now. My fists are my weapons.*

"Sean!" Percy yelled, and he jumped back, grabbing Sean and jumping up a flight of stairs. "You okay?" Sean started dragging his feet next to Percy's upstairs, pursued by face creatures yelling at the top of their lungs.

One of the creature's arms stretched out and swung toward the group.

Melody put up her forearms and kicked at the creature with her right leg. She then crossed her arms and ran forward, and cut the creature in half with her hand.

"Thanks for that," Percy said, getting up from the ground with the other two.

"Look up there," Melody pointed.

The group of four looked at a solid door.

"It could be a trap," Percy said, "but it's where we have to go." Percy ran forward up the flight of stairs, with everyone following behind him. "Come on in, hurry up, hurry up," Percy yelled.

Sean saw the hands continue to climb up the cold steel gripping it. "We want it now," the voices screamed. Sean felt unsteady running up the stairs.

Melody leaped forward as one of her legs fell through a wooden step.

"I got you," Sean said as he ran up behind her and grabbed her hand, lifting her up before one of the shadows dragged her through the floorboard.

"Thank you," Melody gasped, holding him tight as they ran hand-in-hand.

Percy was the first at the door. He pulled it open. "Go now, Faye."

Faye nodded as she ran in, followed quickly by Sean and Melody.

Percy's gaze darted across the pitch-black space, where the stairwell was about to vanish. He entered and shut the door behind him a group of charcoal hands almost gripping his neck.

Chapter 17

Percy took a moment to catch his breath and look back at his three underlings. "You guys, okay?"

"Define okay," Melody murmured as she sat there, her breath heavy. "Almost got taken out by a giant black hand. It was unnerving to see faceless beings with gigantic arms swinging at us. First a big flower and now this, but y'all said anything like this could happen in the dreamscape. So I need to take a moment and breathe."

"Sense anything?" Percy asked Faye.

"Demons were bouncing all over the place. It's like I can't really pinpoint it. I feel sorrow." Faye brushed her hand on the oak painted wall.

Sean took a glance around and saw what seemed to be a lengthy file of clocks.

"We appear to be in a shop of sorts," Melody stated.

Sean looked around and saw a makeshift shop of clocks. One was a swirl of gray that seemed gloomy and damned. He took a peek up at the ceiling. Chandeliers of gold spinning in circles and back and forth to the left and right. "I'm glad we made it out of there. I sure thought we were going to die. Did you see what I did? I was able to use my power."

"We did see you throw punches," the group said.

"It's exciting to know how you can manifest your power. When I first used my fist, it was exciting to see how it all played out. It's great to train, but you have to learn to master your power. You need to spend a bit more time with me," Faye asserted.

Sean nodded, and he looked out at the chandeliers, which were twirling a bit slower now.

"Does anyone sense anything?" Percy asked. He stepped up to the cabinet and took a closer look at the tiny cash register that was within. Money was appearing in dollar bills and disappearing as the door opened and closed.

Paintings adorned the walls. Some looked like they were famous people others were not so elegant, like a janitor holding a giant clock or a woman adorned in crown jewels.

Faye cautiously avoided the crevices in the hardwood flooring for fear of setting off a trap. "You would think this man may owe these people money, or perhaps he was so famous they wanted more handcrafted watches."

They looked up at the paintings, each one putting their hands right up to feel if it was moving about.

"That makes sense," Melody stated "these paintings are repeating the word 'give'. Maybe they want so much of him they demanded his soul."

"I don't know about that," Sean said. "If he lost his soul, why live in such a modest house? If you lost your soul, your house would be filled up with possessions. We saw more of a familial home."

"Good catch," Percy said, "I was thinking the same thing. Though you can never be too sure about dreams, loss, and love. The manifestations of a person's heart take place in the dreamscape. Apparently, this shop was essential to him, and it was luxurious at one point."

"Dreams are where a person's innermost thoughts and feelings come to life. Do you think someone tried to buy him out?" Faye asked.

"It's possible," Percy said, walking toward the front of the shop. "Everyone, come here," he said.

The remaining three hurried along the long shop to the dusty front door that was covered in grime.

Percy wiped the grime off the door on his sleeve. Through the streaks and dust-spotted glass, distant figures were revelated to their eyes.

As they squinted their eyes, the door disappeared, and the shop behind them dissolved as if it was a distant memory.

"What happened?" Sean looked below him, and he saw gray metal and iron bars.

Before them, giant pendulums swung back and forth.

Sean looked at the darkness below them, which covered the entire floor. *Don't think I want to go there.* He tapped his back pocket, feeling the letter from Tabatha.

Faye walked forward, looking back at everyone. "I will go first."

Percy nodded and looked at her, smiling. "You got this."

Faye grinned and moved closer to the platform's edge. She knelt and leaped over the gap to the first pendulum.

"Whoa," Faye said, wobbling slowly. She bent, feeling the wind across her face. It smelled like sawdust. She jumped over to the next pendulum, which was slightly higher.

Percy glanced back at Melody and Sean. "Go ahead, you two."

Sean looked at Melody; his eyes widened slightly. "Let's go! I'm scared. My balance is horrible."

"Trust me," Melody said, looking at him with a sincere glance. She grabbed his hand and leaped into the air.

Sean gripped his hand tight in hers as she landed on the middle of the pendulum.

"Whoa," Sean said, shifting back almost sliding off the side of the giant golden circle.

"I got you!" Melody shifted her weight back, saving him from certain death.

"How are you able to do that?" Sean looked at her with a puzzled look.

"I used to be a gymnast," she said, her large glasses bouncing slightly. As Melody regained her footing, she clung to Sean's arm with both hands.

Sean's eyes stayed fixed on hers. *I guess that explains her dexterity and ability to keep her balance. That darkness below would be consuming if it was not for her.*

Melody nodded, and she gripped his hand harder. "Here we go to the second one; we need to catch up to Faye."

Sean looked around, and he saw four to five more pendulums swing back and forth. "You got that, Percy?" Percy gave him a slight nod. He felt reassured in his spirit.

Melody gripped Sean's hand, and she jumped up into the air toward the next pendulum, which was slightly higher. Her feet slipped as she was stabilizing Sean and maintained her balance.

"You okay?" she asked. "We are almost halfway there." Melody looked around above a few solid numbers illuminating the giant clock tower from the window. The sunshine streamed through, revealing dust swirling around the upper section. She shielded her eyes, looking up at the next pendulum. "We have three more to go, and Faye is already on the other side."

Wow, she's fit. "Well, I didn't tell you I'm terrified of heights. That's why I would never fly in an airplane of any sort, but I don't mind gliding with you," Sean said.

Melody blushed slightly as she stood up, gripping Sean. The two of them jumped across to the third pendulum, which was a straight shot across a small gap.

"You guys hurry up," Faye yelled. "I see something up ahead; get with it. I can't wait all day."

"I don't know if she hates me or likes me, or something in between," Sean told Melody.

"She cooks for you. She probably likes you as a friend." Melody looked at the pendulum, which was below them.

Melody jumped again and felt like they were going at least 100 feet. They landed gracefully on the pendulum below them.

"I was scared to death, but I jumped," Sean said. *I didn't die. It feels like we were going forever. How did we not die?*

"The one thing my Guardian Angel taught me is to understand the flow of mana in the dreamscape." Melody put her arms around Sean, holding him tightly as the pendulum swung back and forth. "On Earth, yes, we would probably have broken knees and ankles. But we are in a dream world, and we can reshape the way we land to mitigate the pain of landing."

"Yeah, my legs are a bit sore, but it's not overwhelming. It is much like a swell of my heart, like riding a roller coaster of sorts. It felt like fun, too but also terrifying. I feel comforted as well. Could you hold my hand so I don't fall into the darkness?"

Melody giggled and gripped his hand, rubbing her index finger across it.

Sean felt a rush of emotion as he looked into Melody's eyes for a moment smiling. "Thank you for explaining that to me. I need to think like a spiritual being now," Sean stated. "If I try to understand this place and the Dreamweaver Society with my human mind from the earth, nothing will make sense, and I will limit myself."

"You are starting to sound like one of the uppers," Melody said. "I can see why Elijah took a liking to you."

Sean nodded as he focused on the pendulum above them.

Percy waved toward Sean and Melody, who were below him. "Guys, are you okay? It looks like your handing it okay," he yelled to Melody.

"No, I was ready for the task," she yelled up. "Sean is doing all right."

"It looks like you've had a lot of it," Percy said, giggling slightly. "You two hurry up, we're almost there, and I can see Faye's eyes staring at you now."

Melody nodded back. She sat there looking up. *I can do this. I can't let Sean know how much I'm hurting. He's heavy!* Melody took a deep breath jumped into the air.

Without skipping a beat, Sean felt his legs touch the last pendulum and leaped over a little space where Faye was standing.

"It is way too much," Faye proclaimed, walking over to Sean patting him on the shoulder. "A bit much for a newbie," she said.

Melody is a newbie as well. Sean cast a peek across at Melody, whose hand he was still holding. *This feels nice.* He started to daydream and let go of her hand. *I have to keep focus. I can't fall for another woman.* "I didn't hold your hand too tight, did I?" Sean asked Melody.

"No, no, it's okay. I wanted to make sure you had a good grip. No, I am a little bit exhausted as well. Melody took a seat on the ground leaning against the cold steel."

"You probably don't have too long to sit," Faye said. "Percy is already coming this way."

"I'll take what I can get." Lifting a man of Sean's caliber across five pendulums took a lot of strength. She knew how to use focus energy

Sean turned his attention to the long hallway in front of them. It was twisted and had the appearance of a kaleidoscope of colors moving at the same time. He wanted to walk forward, but he knew he needed to wait for Faye and the others, but his curiosity piqued. *What if it was an illusion? What if there was some sort of trap? I need to warn them.*

"Sorry to keep you waiting," Percy said, and he jumped up from the last pendulum. Percy wiped the dust off his suit as he walked forward, looking at Melody, who was soaked in sweat near the edge of the platform. "You did good," he said, putting his fist out to her.

Melody looked up, wiped her glasses slightly with her shirt. "Thank you! Sean was heavy, though." The human woman put her fist up to meet Percy's.

Sean turned around, scratching the edge of his chin. He looked at her with a smile. "Sorry about that. I had a lot to eat."

"You are talking about the meals I cooked for you because I was nice. I don't want you to eat my food anymore. I did it to show you I will be kind to you." Faye stormed up to Sean.

Sean put up his hands, waving them frantically. "Don't worry, I am not talking about your food. I tend to stress eat at times," he proclaimed.

"Do you need to hit the gym?" Faye said.

Before Sean could answer, the clock tower shook violently. The pendulum behind them started to sway as if becoming unhooked.

Melody let out a slight squeak as she stood up, trying to steady herself. "What is that?" she asked.

"It's what we like to call a shift," Percy said. "The old man may be waking up, so we need to hurry."

"What happens if we get trapped in here?" Sean blurted.

"That could happen," Percy affirmed. "But we have a mission, and we had to save this man from his fate. Everyone, follow me," he said.

Percy ran forward to the colorful swirling hallway.

He didn't answer my question! Sean was in the middle and looking back at Melody, he lost his balance, but he kept running forward, breathing heavily onward on the pathway.

201

The hallway shook as if being inside an earthquake.

"Whoa!" Melody screamed as was swung back, sliding down the hallway.

"I got you!" Faye dashed back, grabbing Melody's hand pulling her up from the trembling floor below them.

The group came toward a dead end. Percy looked up at the walls above a bright light of sorts shining through. "We could jump to the wall sketch."

Sean thought back to the training he had where he was leaping across the wall gaps. *The shaking is really starting to piss me off!*

Percy turned his gaze back at Melody and Sean. "Sean jump on my back and Melody on Faye's back. Let's go!"

Sean ran over without hesitation then jumped on the back of his leader. At a moment's notice, they were going back and forth between the walls in about a 5-foot gap. The vertical walls seem to last for an eternity.

Percy jumped against the last side of the wall and landed at a stairwell leading up toward the roof of the clock tower.

"Off you go," Percy asserted in a kind tone. Percy bent on one knee, putting his hand out to Sean lifting him up.

"Who was your mentor?" Sean put his hand on Percy's shoulder.

"Well," Percy panted with a smile. Before Percy could finish his sentence, Sean felt his body slamming to the side of the narrow hallway.

"Percy," Sean screamed as he reached for his hand. Sean stretched out, but he was unable to grasp his friend's hand. A claw of sorts manifested into Percy's shoulder. Before Sean could respond, the experienced blonde Dreamweaver's body vanished up the stairs.

Chapter 18

Sean bolted up the stairs to see Percy slam hard into the ground. "Percy!" Sean gasped, and he took a step out onto what he saw below him. His eyes traced the two big clock hands spiraling around the clock. Percy was on his back, blood running up his arm, his body moved, twitching. "Are you okay? Percy, speak to me."

"It's a bit of a flesh wound. Nothing too bad," he said, sitting up. Percy looked over at Sean, giving him a thumbs-up as he grabbed his sword and stood up slowly. "Stay back!" he bellowed.

Sean noticed the hands of the clock, and his eyes met the creature standing in the middle of the clock towers squelette hands. The animal was standing there with three eyes. It had long circular arms, and its hands were pincers. There was a small metal stick in its arms.

Faye ran up beside Sean. "Percy," she yelled. As she leaped into the air, her leg glowed yellow. She kicked at the demon several times. Her leg smacked it in the head and again in the chest. She pulled her fist back and uppercut it into the air ten feet.

"You Dreamweaver's are so cocky." The demon cackled. It backed up, wiping a bit of the blood Faye produced.

Weaving back to the edge of the clock where Percy was standing, she kneeled beside him. She observed his wound. "You're pretty banged up," Faye stated. "It went right through your shoulder. I'm surprised your right arm is still attached."

"Me too," Percy hissed, staring up at her. "I can still fight," he admitted, switching his sword to his left hand as he stood up.

Sean stood there behind Percy and Faye. His fist started to glow green. "How dare you," he muttered underneath his breath. Sean bolted toward the shorthand in the middle of the clock. Leaping into the air, Sean's right hand slammed into the beast's face.

The creature's three eyes looked at Sean. The creature's claws widened and started to close in toward Sean's head.

I'm going to die! Sean felt his life flash before him. Tabatha's smile illuminated his mind. Followed by the warm hand of Melody and the infinite deep gaze of his Guardian Angel.

The beast leaped back at the last second, and a bullet flew over Sean's head.

"Get out of here, Sean," Melody yelled as she cocked the hammer back on her revolver, shooting two more bullets. Boom! Boom! Two more shots rang out toward the creature.

The beast leaped into the air to evade the gunshots before landing beside Percy and Faye.

Faye fell on her back, shocked by the creature's speed.

"Die," Percy yelled. He sprang off the ground, thrusting his blade upward toward the demon's neck.

The demon clamped his two arms in a circular motion before it met its neck. "Too easy," the demon hissed. The monster raises two arms taking Percy into the air with his sword.

Weaving up, Faye twisted to the left and extended her right leg into the stomach of the creature. She cocked her fist back, landing four blows in rapid succession and an elbow to the jaw of the creature.

Percy felt the grip of the blade reeling from Faye's attack. Gripping his sword, he twisted his body and landed right behind the creature. Sword raised, he cut the creature's arm right off with the proper twist of his blade.

"Damn you!" the creature screamed as he took his left arm and smacked Percy in the face slamming him to the ground.

Percy's head hit hard on the wood of the large circular clock.

Faye looked at Percy, whose eyes were white; his body stood still. She looked at her watch, the demonic pressure fluctuating between 15 and 20. *What the hell is happening? The pressure was no more than 4, and this creature should be no more than a 5, but it's on the scale of 20!* "Percy," she uttered slightly as she tried to wake her friend.

Sean looked over and saw Percy's body lifeless on the ground. "Percy!" he yelled as he ran over to his friend's limp body.

"You two better leave now!" Faye protested.

"What about Percy?" Melody started to reload her gun. She knew her mana was too drained to manifest more bullets.

The demon leaped back on the other side of the giant clock and stood there. "This man's soul is mine. You shall not have it!"

"Help me, please!" the old man bellowed.

The group of three glanced up to find the old man above them caught in gold and black suspension chains snaking around his arms and dragging his limbs in every way.

"You wouldn't dare leave this old man here for me to torture him," the demon said, his three eyes blinked quickly in each direction. "I am going to rip him limb from limb, you know. There will be nothing of his soul left; he will go to The Void. It is a Dreamweaver's job to kill us, right? If you kill me, I'll kill him." The demon let go of a cackle and stood there hunched over his right arm.

"I need to get Percy to a safe place," Faye said. "We also have to save this man." She looked up at the man above, who had chains around his neck, his wrists, and his ankles. *I can't leave him! But also, I need to protect Sean and Melody. If I fall, they will die. I have no choice.*

Faye put her hands behind her head, and she twisted her long black ponytail. "Time to get serious. You have to dig deep, Melody, and try to manifest more bullets! I am counting on you! Shoot when I tell you, Melody. Sean, get Percy out of the line of attack."

Melody nodded, breathing heavily, and she closed her eyes, trying to concentrate.

Sean leaped over to where Percy was and lifted him up slowly. *Man, he lost a lot of blood.* Sean looked at him, and he started to walk around the outer circle of the clock face.

Faye walked forward, looking straight at the demon. "I'm a Dreamweaver, and I'm here to help those who can't fight for themselves in the spiritual realm! You will fall before me!" she roared.

"Call me Tiberius," the demon dictated, writhing in pain as his right arm continued to regrow. "I am the one who sees all, and what I see are a bunch of chumps. I see those who are scared of what I can do. Your friend got a cheap shot in, but I will not be fooled again. I already know all of your moves; I can see everything." Another eye appeared from the left side of the demon body and one on the right side. Two more appeared at the bottom of the chin and above his head. The demon cackled. "You will fall before me." His arm re-grew, and he lunged toward Faye.

Faye took a step back and snapped her fingers. A set of nunchucks appeared in each hand. They were brown with black handles.

Tiberius closed in on Faye, and he put both of his arms out, aiming toward her for the head.

Faye anticipated the onslaught and swung one nunchuck, the other shielding the hits. She and Tiberius were locked back and forth. She turned to the left, and he swung to the right. She ducked, dodging an attack. The demon lifted both of his arms, slamming toward Faye. She put her weapons together, blocked the attack, and she felt the pressure of the demon's force on her. She went on her knees, slowly feeling them give way. Screaming, she pushed back up, negating the attack. Her weapons disappeared as she interlocked her arms behind the demon's head. She pulled back her right leg and slammed her knee into its chin.

"How are you able to hit me?" Tiberius screamed. "My eyes can't trace you; what type of trickery is this?

"Wouldn't you like to know?" Faye said, and she snapped both of her fingers toward the demon, her chucks appeared, and she ran forward, smacking Tiberius in the face to the left and to the right up and across his body as hard as she could.

Melody opened her eyes. "I can't even follow them; they fight so quick," Melody said. "She told me to fire when she says so." Looking down at her hand, she had two bullets red in color ready to go. "Faye can't keep on fighting like that forever."

Sean brought Percy over to Melody, who was crouched by the stairs entrance. He laid his friend on the ground wiping blood off Percy's head.

"We have to do this," Melody told Sean looking at him with intense eyes.

Sean looked over to Faye, who was charging toward the creature keeping up with its intense strikes. "They are moving so fast. If we tried to interfere, we would cause problems."

"I saw his eyes pop out of his head. He seems to be on the defense now. I think she is trying to skew his vision in a way." Melody's hands were shaking violently as she looked back at the creature who was battling Faye.

"I have an idea," Sean insisted, looking over at Melody.

"Faye told me to stay put," Melody yelled.

"The way she is moving, I don't think Faye can keep it up. That monstrosity can regenerate. We need to find a way to distract it." Sean's eyes bounced around the trying to catch his thoughts.

Melody's eyes focused on the man who was screaming above the clock's face. "What did you have in mind?"

"Take a shot at the man's chains," Sean said. "I am going to run to help Faye."

"Don't get killed," Melody stated, with tears flowing through her eyes.

As he dug his legs into the payment, Sean nodded, and he jumped on the first clock hand toward the battle.

"Stay back!" Faye screamed.

"You should listen to your superior," Tiberius yelled. The demon whipped back his arms, and he smacked Faye, who was distracted by Sean running toward him.

Sean charged forward, jumping over the creature interlocking his arms around the demon's legs.

"What a foolish attempt!" Tiberius bellowed.

"Do it, Melody!" Sean looked over at her with an intense glare in his eyes. He felt his arms start to buckle as the demon started to spread his legs.

Melody's hands trembled. *I can do this!* She cocked her handgun back, loaded two rounds into it, and aimed toward the man's shackles. Her finger slipped into the trigger's grip. BOOM! BOOM!

Melody collapsed to her knees, drained by the mana she had expended.

"You guys are both idiots," Faye said, studying her balance; she looked at the creature who was looking up at the bullets going toward the old man suffering.

Letting out a cackling scream, Faye ran forward and wrapped her nunchucks around the creature's neck.

"This can't be happening." The creature put out his arms, pushing them toward the neck of the experienced Dreamweaver.

Faye, with her hands glowing yellow, connected the new chucks and pulled with all her might.

When the bone snapped, a loud crack could be heard across the room. The demon's head broke off, spraying blood over both Sean and Faye.

The bullets reigned in, hitting the chains, and the man slowly fell toward the ground.

"You think you can kill me Tiberius yelled as his head started to fall back toward his body. I am all—"

"Then watch this!" Melody, on the ground, exhausted from her attacks from earlier, rained out more bullets at an immense speed.

"No, this can't be happening!" Tiberius screamed.

The bullets struck the demon's skull, bursting on contact.

Sean peered up as the man's body was reaching the ground. He leaped up intuitively to his arms, feeling as if he were made of rubber. He reached out his hands, seizing the weak old guy and lowering him to the ground.

Faye, exhausted, lay on her back, breathing heavily. "What the hell," she proclaimed, and she rolled, looking over at Sean. "You did well. That was stupid, but you did well."

The frail old man began to move. He stood up, danced, his legs moved back and forth, his arms swinging in a circle as if he had his favorite song on his mind.

"Thank you for saving me. I don't know what I would've done if I didn't have people like you to battle evil for those cannot."

"No problem," Sean and Faye said in unison as they put their thumbs up, exhausted from the fight that transpired.

The clock tower was filled with a bright white that seemed to emerge out of nowhere. The sky above them was covered with white clouds.

"You have done well," a female voice said, "now join your wife in paradise."

The man looked up at the sky, his eyes wide as he saw the face of his wife appear before him. He started to float into the air slowly. He looked back at the group of four who had fought on his behalf. "Thank you," he said.

The female voice spoke once more. "My Dreamweaver's, I pray you feel my love. Work hard and earn your salvation."

Sean immediately felt his body filled with the greatest love he'd ever known; he fell on his face at the power of the voice. *What is this? It's this who I think it is? Is this the goddess?* Before Sean could comprehend what was happening, the presence was gone, and a brilliant white light filled the room once again in the house of the old watchmaker.

Melody, Faye, and Sean all started at each other with tears in their eyes.

"I've never heard her voice," Faye said as she touched her head, tears streaming from her eyes. "It was so sweet. It was the best thing I've ever heard. I can't describe it."

"It's what we were fighting for. We put our souls on the line for this ultimate peace. I've never felt so happy before." Melody sat up on her knees, her hands covering her face.

Sean stood up, limping over to Faye. "I remember growing up and hearing people talk about Ananastia's love. Those with a spiritual connection to her would study the ancient text. I didn't believe at the time, but to hear her speak was like the deepest part of my soul trembled with joy."

"Don't forget about me." Percy winced as he sat up.

Faye rushed over on her knees, putting Percy's head on her lap. "You should not be speaking, I thought you were going to die. We need to get you back up quickly to be healed."

Percy put his hands on his chest. "I think I was touched, and the wound healed up, but it hurts. It hurts so bad. Did you get him?"

"Yeah, we saved him, and he is in paradise now with his wife and the goddess." Faye gazed at Percy, tears streaming down her cheeks, hitting his face.

"Sounds good. I'm going to sleep now." Percy closed his eyes and drifted off to sleep.

Faye looked at Percy, who was on her knees. "We got you, friend," she whispered. "All right, Sean, put Percy on my back. Melody, help him up as well."

Melody and Sean lifted Percy up, and Faye bent on her knees. She looked at her watch, glowing a bright orange showing there was a way back home nearby.

Melody looked as well. "It seems we have to travel half a mile."

Faye strolled toward the door with Percy on her back. Sweat poured on her face, but she stepped forward with her friend on her back.

"I'm surprised we lived through that." Melody strolled beside Faye.

The sun was starting to rise from the sky. The lake beside the old man's house glistened.

"I knew we were going to make it," Faye said. "It's all about stamina and power. If you have those two things and a positive outlook, you can overcome anything."

"I think this is the wisest thing you have said thus far," Sean remarked.

Faye didn't answer or glance back at Sean but instead continued forward.

Perhaps she's too exhausted for banter. Sean slowed his pace trailing behind Faye.

Up in the distance, the group of three saw the golden tornado spiral up toward the heavens.

"Almost there, Percy. Hang on," Faye whispered.

The group went up the small staircase with Melody spotting Faye as they approached the golden cyclone.

Sean walked up beside Faye with a smile on his face. Let me help. Sean bent as Faye and Melody transferred Percy on his back.

Sean walked forward, closed his eyes. The warmth of the magical cyclone enveloped him as he floated above the ground.

Chapter 19

Later that morning...

Sean walked into the room as Faye and Melody sat there surrounded by friends and fellow onlookers.

"Hey," Melody whispered, coming up and giving Sean a big hug. "Were you able to clean up?"

The young nurse with long blonde hair and pink eyes stood over Percy, her hands glowing a deep blue like the ocean. She looked back at everybody in the room. "I've done everything I could do."

"That's a load of bull," Faye yelled. "You say nothing can be done?"

The nurse turned around, walked straight, and looked Faye in the eye. "There is still so much we don't know. We continue to do good; the other side continues to do evil. Sadly, he is a casualty of war. Make sure you report everything you know about the situation. Sorry, everyone."

"What happened?" Sean asked, walking up to Faye and putting his hand on her shoulder.

Before Faye could answer, a familiar voice rang through as a gentleman walked through the door.

"Look, it is everybody's favorite arrogant prick," Faye snapped. Her eyes cut a glance toward the door sliding open.

"That is no way to treat a friend," Eric said. The gentleman strode in his long blue robe and white suit, illuminating the room as if he was the star of the show.

"Why are you here?" Faye asked.

Eric brushed his blonde hair back. "I heard my dear friend was in trouble, and I came to make certain of his status. Also, I heard you found an anomaly. You were beat up pretty bad."

"It was a tough battle," Faye said, "but you care nothing for Percy. You've always found him to be your rival." Faye stormed up to the blonde Dreamweaver, looking him straight in his eye.

"I am also here to get information. I am to lead investigation on these anomalies and these syphers. I was sent into the field to study them. Any information you can give me will help me track them and understand their power." Eric took a step forward, his head nearly touching Faye's.

Faye backed off, and she walked over, sitting next to Percy, who was still asleep.

"Is it true?" Eric asked, walking up to look at Percy resting in the bed. "Can he no longer use mana energy?"

"If you heard what the nurse said, then yes, it is true he can no longer use mana. His loss is his ability as a Dreamweaver. Something about that anomaly changed or altered his blood flow. It tainted his mana. He can't fight anymore!"

"The demons have found a way to taint a Dreamweaver's energy flow. This is devastating. I am sorry." Eric let out a slight smirk along with his condolences. "What other information do you have?"

"I don't feel like talking to you anymore," Faye said, her eyes concentrated on Percy.

"What about these two? I remember you, Sean. I saved you when you were studying how to be more elegant."

"I don't know what that means," Sean said. "But I agree with Faye. I don't want to talk either. I want to be with my friend, and I want to grieve."

"You do know withholding information is a punishable offense." Eric crossed his arms and turned around.

"Don't worry, we'll get it on public record," Faye stated, looking back at him. "You will have all the information you can go through. Now leave!"

Eric looked back one more time, cutting a glance at Percy as he walked through the door.

"He gives me the creeps," Melody gulped. "That man is so full of himself."

"Eventually, you learn to ignore him," Faye said, and she put her hands in the hands of Percy. "You two need to get some rest. I will watch over him."

"But…" Sean inquired, clutching his fists looking at her.

"What we all went through was very traumatic. Get some rest, don't worry about the report. I'm going to take care of it. Now go, it's an order." Faye turned her attention back to Percy. Sean and Melody walked out of the room.

"You know she's right," Melody said. "We need to get some rest. You want a ride back to your place?"

"Yeah, sounds good. Thanks," Sean said as he followed her toward her broom, wrapping his arms around her.

Her embrace. She is so warm. He put his hand in his back pocket. He thought of the letter from Tabatha. *How can I fall for another woman when I am also seeking the one I lost? She's right in front of me. She's perfect. She's sexy. She smells excellent. She doesn't think less of me. Tabatha always looked down on me. Melody's carefree spirit is a breath of fresh hair.*

Sean was lost in thought. Before he knew it, they were at the front steps of his door.

"Do you need time alone, or would you like some company? We could play a game or go get a massage. Oh, maybe fried shrimp?" Melody's eyes looked hopeful yet held a deep sense of sorrow.

"I'm okay. I think I will go to take a nap." Sean started to turn around and walk toward his door when he felt a tap on the shoulder.

"You know no man needs to be on the island by himself. We are in this together." She went in and gave Sean a slight kiss on the cheek. "It was courageous what you did. I don't think you're a mistake. Don't listen to the people who say otherwise. You're meant to be here. You are here for a reason! Keep pushing! Okay, I'm off. See you maybe tomorrow for lunch or training."

Sean wanted to push forward. He felt his feet instinctively take a move toward Melody, who was standing there with her arms behind her back and her legs slightly crossed. *It's okay to have feelings for another woman. But you have to keep the focus on Tabatha. She is the reason you're pushing so hard. You have to stay focused more on how much you want to move forward and embrace her and hug her. This is a challenging time in your life; you have to keep focus.*

"I wonder if Faye will train with us. It's not like her to stay away for too long." Sean let out a slight giggle as he turned around and went into his house. He looked out his window to see Melody fly off into the air on her broom and disappear from his sight.

He slipped off his shoes, got the letter from his back pocket, and fell on the bed. With one sniff of the letter, he fell into a deep sleep.

Later that night...

Sean woke up when he heard a knock at his door. He looked over at his clock to see it was 1 a.m. in the morning.

"Who in the world will be wanting to talk to me at this time in the morning?" Sean mumbled, wiping his face.

Lifting his body out of bed, he walked over to the door, opened it, and found a letter with a box of cookies with it.

The letter read, "These are your favorite cookies. Join me in the church in thirty minutes. Wear something casual."

This sounds like a date! Cookies and milk at one in the morning. *This handwriting is elegant... probably a female.*

Sean took off his suit and put on a pair of jeans and a t-shirt with a penguin on it. *I need to take a shower, but this can wait.* Sean walked to the station pressing the red button.

Before he knew it, a regular taxi pulled up.

"That will be 500g for a ride. Where are you going?" The cheerful woman's cheeks flared up, holding out her hand, waiting for his card.

"I am heading to the church," Sean stated, reaching in his back pocket to pull out his card.

"I will give you a discount, okay?" The woman put her thumb up, taking the card and pressing it against a small scanner on her watch. "100g because it's late at night. Hop on."

Sean looked at the bird standing before him. It had blue feathers and a prominent brown peak. Its legs were the size of his body.

The bird let out a squawk.

"Whoa, girl," the woman said, patting it on the head. "Hurry up, okay!"

Sean jumped in the back of the brown basket and soon was floating in the air. Sean held on to the bar in the carriage as he felt the bird fly off into the air.

Why does everything have to go so fast? Sean felt the carriage go up in a loop and bolted off across the north, across the Enchanted Sea. *Everything seems to be so extra here!*

The cheerful young woman at the front held onto its feathers. It looked like her hands were dug deep into its skin.

Sean peered over the carriage, his eyes glued to the water. *No matter how many times I see the ocean here, each view is different.* It glowed with a profound, ethereal luminosity. Even at night, you can still see individuals swimming in the sea or floating over the ocean.

Sean felt the gentle breeze whisper across his face.

"Thank you for taking our taxi," the woman said as she looked back at him with a smile guiding the large beast in front of the church.

To the left, Sean shifted his gaze. A beautiful wooden structure with stained glass caught his eye. While the other buildings he had seen were equally impressive, this one had a distinct appeal.

Sean exited the carriage and made his way up the stairwell to the massive wooden structure in front of him. A black and white marble floor with enormous stone pillars leading to the front of the church was all that was visible as he made his way inside. A 40-foot-tall monument of a lady holding a pure gold ring stood in the center of the plaza. She was covered in flowers, and water was flowing from the ground below her. It looked like a place for bathing, but there was nobody there.

In the second row, Sean recognized a familiar face. Walking up, he sat beside a man. He gave him a sideways glance.

"Pretty night for a meeting?" With a grin on his face, Elijah eyed him up and down. "How have you been?"

"It's been crazy, not going to lie," Sean said. "It's frightening to think that if we don't defeat demons, we could be thrown into The Void. I feel like you're someone I can trust, though. I have something to tell you. I got a letter from Tabatha."

Elijah's eyebrows raised. "That was your fiancé, right?

"Yeah, we were supposed to get married in eight months, and then I died. I think about it all the time. This letter, it even smells like her. I know she's out there. Maybe she's in paradise. That is why I have been working so hard. She's been my sole ambition. Where I draw my power and strength from. I focus on her, and I can manfiest my mana. I feel the mana flow through my body. My body comes alive!"

"You have grown a bit. Percy is quite the leader, isn't he?" Elijah leaned back with a smile on his face, glancing up at the ceiling.

"Yeah, he is, but he went through something traumatic, and he may not be able to fight anymore." Sean felt tears swell his eyes as he put his hands on his face. "Can't his powers be restored? Why hasn't Anastasia done anything? Dammit, none of this makes sense."

"I've yet to read anything about what happened to you in your last battle. Right now, I can't really speak about what happened to Percy. I will do my research and see what I come up with. I cannot focus on doom and gloom, and at times what happens in the spiritual realm is beyond our comprehension. You know me, as an intellectual, I do search for the deeper meaning of most things. But there are things I won't understand until I go back and study in the library in the heavens. Information here is limited even as a researcher."

"They are things you don't know," Sean shuttered, looking over at him with tears falling from his eyes, trying not to laugh.

"That's true, but there are also things I don't want to know." Elijah licked his lips. "There are things so scary about this universe, I don't think I could take it. So, I seek the truth to an extent. Once I'm satisfied, I continue on my journey. This leads me to this. I have good news for you."

Sean looked over at the researcher, puzzled by what he heard. "Good news. I could use good news right now."

"Congratulations, Sean, you have been given the rank of under-ranked three Dreamweaver." Elijah pulled out a small box and opened it, showing Sean a bright bronze horizontal bar. Just so you know, this rank goes underneath your suit pocket, or you can put it on your neck collar."

Sean took the small black box started at the bar that showed his reflection.

"Many higher-ups didn't want to give you an actual ceremony because they believe you're not supposed to be here. For your meritorious service, I present to you this rank. Will you continue to help those who can't defend themselves?" Elijah put his hands through his hair, then he stretched his arms out.

"I can't believe it. I actually have a Dreamweaver rank. This is incredible. I'm at a loss for words. After what happened to Percy and everything we've gone through. You have no idea what this means to me. All of my hard work seems to be paying off. Thank you so much for doing this. You breathed new life into my spirit." Sean held the box in his hands as tears of joy streamed down his face. He felt his soul renewed with the vigor to move forward.

"Oh, and there's one more thing. I think it is better, but you read it yourself." Elijah pulled out a small brown envelope and handed it to Sean.

"Hopefully this is more good news," Sean beamed, feeling perky. He opened the letter frantically, but as he read the words, dread filled his spirit.

Elijah sighed his eyes peering down at the dimly lit floor. "This is all I can figure out. It's going to take some time before I can do deeper research. But this is a new lead, and I know this is not what you want to hear. I'm pretty sure it's the truth."

The letter read, "Sean Gillingham. Time of death 8:05 p.m. Murdered by fiancé Tabatha Smith."

"There's no way. There's no way. It has to be a lie," Sean yelled as he stood up in the church. Sean felt his body was going to explode. There's no way she could have killed me. She sent me a letter. She loved me!

Sean dropped the letter as he clutched Elijah on the shoulder. "What do I do? What do I do?"

Sean felt like his soul was being torn apart. He had no idea what hardships awaited him, but all he wanted to know was why the woman he loved murdered him.

www.ingramcontent.com/pod-product-compliance
Lightning Source LLC
Chambersburg PA
CBHW021236130626
46554CB00004B/1523